Distant
Signs

NEEM TREE
PRESS

Anne Richter

Distant Signs

Neem Tree Press Limited, 1st Floor,
2 Woodberry Grove, London, N12 0DR, UK
Published by Neem Tree Press Limited 2019
info@neemtreepress.com

Originally published in German as *Fremde Zeichen*
Copyright © Osburg Verlag GmbH, Hamburg 2013
Translation © Douglas Irving 2019

A catalogue record for this book is available from the British Library

ISBN 978-1-911107-08-8 (hardback)
ISBN 978-1-911107-16-3 (e-book)
ISBN 978-1-911107-09-5 (paperback)

Printed and bound in Great Britain
by Clays Ltd, Elcograf S.p.A.

For Judith

Opening Note

Anne Richter's novel offers a portrait of life in the German Democratic Republic (GDR) as experienced by three generations of two families, including several flashbacks to events before and during the Second World War.

Adolf Hitler's National Socialist German Workers' Party, or Nazi Party, achieved absolute power in Germany in 1933. Under Nazi fascist rule, all opposition elements, including left-wing resistors and communists, were forcibly removed to concentration camps. Later these same camps would become the focus of the systematic persecution of Jewish people under the Nazis' "Final Solution" programme during the Second World War.

In 1945, the victorious allies of the United Kingdom, the United States of America, France and the Soviet Union settled upon a divided governance of post-war Germany. The GDR comprised what had been known since the end of the Second World War as the Soviet Occupation Zone (the "East Zone" referred to early in the novel), and was officially founded as a new state on 7th October 1949. It was one of the Eastern Bloc countries, with close economic, political and ideological ties to the Soviet Union.

During the 1950s, GDR industry was centralised and agriculture collectivised through state-controlled land co-operatives. The emphasis was on labour productivity, and a considerable percentage of the workforce was female. Workers' housing was heavily subsidised and state care provision was high, with freely available childcare.

Pressured by increased production level targets, many GDR citizens chose to emigrate to the West. Between 1949 and 1961 some 2.7 million citizens defected. The Berlin Wall, built in 1961 by the GDR government, was officially an antifascist barrier against the West. In reality, it was a physical barrier to mass defection of GDR citizens, who were closely monitored, both formally and informally, by the state's security police, the infamous Stasi.

By 1965, when *Distant Signs* begins, the GDR continued to emphasise its socialist identity as separate from its capitalist western counterpart, the Federal Republic of Germany (FRG: the "West" referred to by several of the novel's protagonists). In 1971 the GDR declared itself an ideologically distinct socialist state. The ratification of the Basic Treaty between the GDR and the FRG in 1973 led to the two German states recognising each other's sovereignty, and the GDR receiving the international recognition it had sought.

The GDR remained in existence for four decades, until shortly after its fortieth anniversary on 7th October 1989. Soon after, on 9th November, came the fall of the Berlin Wall, possibly the most iconic symbol of the collapse of communism across Eastern Europe. Just under a year later, on 3rd October 1990, the two separate East and West German states were officially reunified. These two closely related historical events are the "momentous changes" mentioned near the end of the novel.

Translator's Note

Words italicised in the original German text have been retained and are generally significant German words, phrases or literary references. In this English language translation further East German cultural or historical terms, as well as general German historical references, are italicised, or else translated into an English equivalent where this exists. These are all marked with the symbol † in the text, and a brief explanation of the term can be found in alphabetical order in an end glossary, for interested readers. Literary references, marked *, appear after the glossary in alphabetical order.

Contents

Contents

Protagonists

Margret

Hans

Sonja, Hans and Margret's daughter

Johanna, Margret's mother

Friedrich, Margret's father

Lene, Hans's mother

Erwin, Hans's father

Communist Cow

Margret • 1965

I ran into my father in the university quadrangle this morning. Our footsteps echoed off the centuries-old walls. He avoided my gaze until we were standing face to face and had looked each other over in embarrassment; finally, he enquired how my exams were going and what plans I had for the semester break. I told him I was planning a short trip with Hans.

The circumspect, impervious nod my father gave no longer provoked my anger; I took it for granted that he neither showed surprise nor asked where we intended to go.

On his forehead, the two familiar lines drew down to his eyes, lending him an air of perpetual contemplation – as a student across from me had once said. My father's meticulous dress reminded me of Marie, the household help who ironed his shirts and ties and straightened his bow ties – of her confidently striding through our house, her gentle groans as she cleaned the bath, and the smell of cleaning products. My father, on the other hand, smelled of sweet tobacco. I shut my eyes and swayed momentarily from the fatigue of nightlong study and because pictures were flooding my memory.

To break the silence, I asked how my mother was. He replied that she was fine. When he cast a furtive glance at his watch, I turned and glanced up at the big university clock tower. My father appeared not to notice. When we said goodbye he offered me his hand, which hung in the air, strangely awkward and limp. His hand was warm, and I could feel the calluses on his fingertips.

∞

Alone again in the courtyard, I scoured the windows for any witnesses to our encounter. Relieved to see none, my gaze drifted farther up to the high midday sky, where a swift circled. I felt dizzy again, so I lowered my eyes to the cobblestones and took a few steps over to the wall. I was accompanied by the fleeting scent of pipe tobacco.

Leaning against the wall I asked myself: what kind of person is he? Last autumn, I had given up hope that my father would acknowledge me as his child, even just pay me any regard, let alone feel anything for me. On my last attempt to entice him from his lair he had leaped out, but only to snarl warily at me, the intruder, chase me off then retreat into his den.

The encounter had begun at one of his cross-faculty lectures, which I attended from time to time. Usually I sat in one of the back rows, but on that day I could only find a seat in the middle of the lecture theatre. My father spoke about the younger generation's duties, here and in West Germany; about books that could help them to fulfil these duties. He said that young people, particularly in the West, had to learn to rebel against their parents' generation and question the fascist past. Most students leaned over their notebooks or stared intently at him. Although I think I know my father's political views well, indeed mostly share them, at that moment I felt the urge to disagree with him.

I assumed my father hadn't yet noticed me, and this seemed to be confirmed when I raised my arm and slowly stood. I was pleased that my presence unsettled him: his smooth, pale facial skin, always clean-shaven, reddened. He turned from the lectern and made for the rear exit, as though he would flee the hall. Just before reaching the door, unexpectedly he turned around, raised his head and, with an imperceptible wave of the hand, invited me to speak. Taken aback, I too turned red and, keeping my eyes trained on the rear exit said that, no matter the circumstances, I was unsure if I would be able to sever all ties with my father. As I hurriedly took my seat again, I sensed the students' stares; then someone clapped, others began to whisper. One student stood up and spoke heatedly about the gas chambers, the concentration camps, the piles of bodies, the silence of the masses. A moment later I felt ashamed of my declaration.

Once the student had finished, my father walked back to the lectern and said in a firm voice, looking directly at one face after another, "In our times, private matters must come second to societal."

A low murmur went through the room; impossible to identify the culprits. It was of no consolation to finally know for certain that my father hadn't simply forgotten me and my sisters, but that his lack of attention corresponded to his Weltanschauung. So, without getting up again, I shouted that he had been braver once, in the past, but soon I faltered because I realised I knew hardly anything about it; there had been a party process, the exact circumstances of which I was unfamiliar with.

My father didn't rise to the bait and resumed his lecture. But because his speech now lacked its usual vigour, the hope grew in me that I had touched a raw nerve; and on my way home this hope remained stronger than every other feeling. Yet the more I thought about it, the more inappropriate my behaviour during the lecture now seemed.

One evening several days later, there were two rings at my door. Over recent days I had hoped with every ring that there would be a second, because two rings was our family signal: when I forgot my key as a schoolgirl, or when on occasion I visited my parents in my first years at university, they knew by the two rings that there was no need to get changed or clear the dirty coffee cups from the table or quickly open the window to get rid of the smell of food.

By the time he had climbed the stairs my father had cast off his stiffness and his thoughtful expression. I smiled and invited him in, nervous but pleased he had found the way to my flat. Without looking round, he went through the hall into my tiny kitchen and sat on the stool I pushed over to him, the only padded one I had. I offered him bread, and wine or lemonade, but he said he wished to make it brief: he asked that I not interfere in his professional affairs; if I were interested in philosophy, then he was glad, but it had hardly been about philosophy, rather, about me affronting him in front of the others; why, that was unclear to him – had it to do with my mother? Did I blame him for her illness?

I fluctuated between dismay and a remaining glimmer of hope that dwindled by the second as our silence filled the room and I considered what he had just said. Talking, I thought despairingly, would no longer help us.

∞

When I was little I had two mothers: my biological one and my big sister, Rosa, who comforted me when my mother couldn't stand my screaming, gave me food from her plate after my mother had shared it all out, and carried me to the air-raid shelter while my mother took our sister Tanya by piggyback.

Rosa was thin and reached almost to my mother's shoulders. She never cried; she didn't laugh or shout. After the war, once my father was living with us again (and Rosa had reached my mother's chin), sometimes she ran over to him and buried her face in his grey woollen jacket. Briefly he stroked her dark hair and gently pushed her away.

My father wore the jacket summer and winter. When he laid it over the back of the rough living-room armchair or left it in the bathroom, I too sometimes sniffed at the itchy wool, redolent of pipe tobacco.

When we moved into a detached house a few years later, my father placed the armchair in his new study. If he got too warm during a meal he would stand up, cross over to his study and return without his jacket. Only once did I discover it on the hook on the back door that led into our garden. My father took his strolls there. That March day it was warmer out than in. As I walked past I discreetly fingered the wool.

My mother found the house far too large. My father needed a room for his library; he had taken up a professorship at the university and earned well. So my mother insisted upon engaging a gardener and a household help. During the day my mother mostly lay on the sofa and would only get up to give the housekeeper money for the shopping, or to remind Tanya and me of our homework.

We avoided confrontation with our mother because we feared her raised voice. On one of his visits, the family doctor admonished us, "Your mother has to look after herself; she has a weak heart."

Tanya and I nodded shamefacedly. A few days later, Tanya pressed her hand up to my left, still-flat breast, and I pressed my hand to one side of the slight bump she had in the same place.

"My heart's stronger than yours – can you hear?" I giggled.

"You have to put your hand right on top," Tanya replied, but I didn't dare. We were crouched behind a hazelnut bush at the bottom of the garden, where we often played in the hope that no one would hear us.

Sometimes, while Tanya and I chased squirrels or played catch, Rosa would lean against the house wall and gaze in the direction of some far-off tree she scarcely seemed to see. Only when my father opened his office window half a metre away and called for quiet, or when my mother came to the door and shouted, "Is Marie to do all the work herself?" or, "How does the upstairs bathroom look?" or, "Come and sweep the stairs!" did Rosa give a start and totter into the house on her spindly legs. Tanya and I hid behind the hazelnut bush and from there watched what went on behind the windows.

From one day to the next, Rosa left us. She ran off after a haggard military doctor, whose erratic behaviour Tanya and I had often laughed about. Although I had rarely played with Rosa, I missed her greatly. Even though latterly she had glided shadow-like through the house, suddenly I felt as though the absence of that shadow had robbed me of a safeguard without which I felt anxious and insecure; I could always go to Rosa when someone from school taunted me, or if I felt sad for no apparent reason.

After Rosa moved out, I went along with my parents' suggestion that I attend boarding school from ninth grade. My decision was made easier by the knowledge that Tanya would be there as of autumn, and I, following on two years later, would be sure to have her near when I started; besides, Free School Community† sounded like a place where no one complained about noisy games or laughter.

Tanya and I no longer played catch. She brought home friends with whom she whispered behind her hand, and I joined in their roaring laughter without knowing the reason for it. Our sudden outbursts, lasting minutes at a time, disturbed my father at his work and unnerved my mother, with the result that Tanya's friends gradually stayed away and eventually Tanya longed to move out.

∞

To reach my boarding school, first you go by train over the flat then by bus up to villages scattered amongst extensive forest; from the bus stop at the forest edge you walk along the village street then turn right into the school grounds. Every September, villagers crane their necks to see the new pupils, but they also slip them food (sausage and honey), the boys schnapps and cigarettes. Tanya had a boyfriend in the Young Patriot house who used to meet up secretly with other boys to play cards; she told me how she would often see them furtively sucking peppermints the next morning and turning their heads aside when talking with the teachers or senior house boys.

I lived in Red Flag, a small house with a bell tower. Today I would perhaps find the bell's dull ring pleasant, but each school morning it wrenched me awake with a start. Before we assembled in the school yard for morning roll call, we had ten minutes to brush our teeth, wash and dress, and fifteen for breakfast.

I didn't mind the confines of the six-bed dormitory. We chatted and played music together, made fun of each other's idiosyncrasies without hurting each other (no one here called me a "communist cow", like they had at my old school). We worked in the fields and the henhouse, in summer bathed in the chilly pond close by, gathered mushrooms in the shaded woods or on winter evenings appeared in the dining hall where our teachers, sitting in our midst, spoke softer than in class. The fire in the middle of the hall spread a cosy warmth to the farthest row of seats. On other evenings, when I sought peace and wished to be alone, I withdrew to the boarding-school library. As soon as I opened a book and became immersed in the narrative, I experienced a strange captivating thrill; I lost myself in the story and only became aware of my surroundings again when the librarian came to check the aisles and told the last remaining readers to leave.

I had little to do with Tanya. Sometimes we met in the playground or the hall and briefly messed around before going back to our own friends.

∞

At first I made regular visits home. No sooner would I arrive than my mother would reproach me for my dirty clothes and the additional work I caused her, but at the same time for my sporadic visits. She complained about her tiredness, her head and joint pain, and that she was limited in many ways. My father I only got to see at mealtimes, and when I arrived and left.

Together with Marie I washed my own and my parents' clothes; I cajoled my mother to take walks, rubbed ointment into her joints and back, and brushed aside the disconcerting sensation triggered by the sight and touch of her soft swollen body.

Back at boarding school I always reproached myself for not devoting more time to my mother. Once, I spoke about this to Tanya, who nonchalantly replied that it was not our problem. I did not like her saying that, and, although I felt reluctant to go home more often than necessary, still I went time and again.

One day – it was in my final year – I received a letter from my father, the first in the four years I had been at boarding school. At the time I didn't yet know what I was going to study; I was interested in plants and liked to look up their names, their significance and uses, but I also liked being with people and was intrigued by the influence our teacher exerted over me. It struck me as very fulfilling to educate children or young people who would work alongside each other in harmony and exist in a happy community like ours.

My father wrote that he and my mother wished me to complete a period of practical work before beginning my studies, because contact with workers or farmers in our state was an important experience, one they had unfortunately not been able to impart to me; in addition, I would make a personal contribution to the country's economic development.

I pictured my father's slender hands, which he had once run over the bark of a tree, or the time he had clumsily cut a flower from the garden with secateurs to put in a tumbler on his writing desk; I saw his fingers deftly tapping at his typewriter, his eyes inflamed from reading, the lines on his forehead. That aside, I found his sudden interest in my development strange; however, it was probably only about me insofar as I, a part of the community, had a duty to fulfil, the sense of which was clear to me.

ૐ

To mark our school-leaving I went with some of the girls to the coast for two weeks. On our return, we gave each other long hugs at the train station before going our separate ways. I took the tram and got out not far from our house. The closer I drew to my parents' house, the clearer I heard my mother's voice. I opened the garden gate and walked up to the kitchen window in the hope that someone might notice me. My mother was standing not a metre from my father, shouting in his face; suddenly, she stroked his cheeks and his hair, before breaking into sobs and sinking into a chair; my father spoke softly to her, without touching her. I would gladly have turned and fled the scene. Even though I had known these scenarios from childhood, the sight of my parents pained me unexpectedly; at the same time, I wanted to understand what was going on between them.

But my parents barely spoke with me during the following weeks. My father had found me a placement on a farm, as I had requested. The training farm belonged to the university and comprised countless fields and meadows. I knew the village directly bordering the city from walks and had observed how the corn glinted in the sun one last time before harvest, how the cows peacefully grazed and the horses pulled trailers of harvested crops along the village street towards the farmyard. The farmers either nodded affably to us walkers or ignored us.

In early August the late summer air lay hot and oppressive; the village street was lined with horse droppings. At the farm gate I encountered a girl leading a horse under the archway through a sawdust-filled trough. There was a strong smell of disinfectant. The girl briefly studied my clothes and told me I had to thoroughly clean my shoes – that there was foot-and-mouth.

My shoes sank deep into the wet sawdust, which clung to the hem of my woollen skirt. In the yard I sat on a wooden bench under a small linden and picked off the sawdust. Several young people in wellington boots and dirty blue dungarees, probably trainees, walked past me and smirked. Only later did I work out that it was because I was the daughter of an academic.

∽

There were some days when I almost gave up. I was used to the early rising, but I found the strenuous physical work hard; it hardly compared with our afternoon farming activities at school when we had dug potatoes or turnips, fed the hens and planted out flowerbeds.

But it felt good in the evenings as the pain subsided in my joints, and the strain eased from the dung cart against my stomach and the weight of the potato baskets on my forearms. I got used to seeing the ends of my fingernails brown – they looked eerie in the moonlight – but the work in the fields and the byre demanded the utmost of me; still, my strength seemed to suffice, until that day in mid-September.

I had been assigned to clear rogue shoots along with some of the farm girls, as well as the girls from my dorm who were studying agriculture. We were standing in the middle of a field in two long lines at the edges of a hand-scythed strip, each facing an uncut side of the field. I saw the golden-green flower stems before me and knew that they contained valuable seeds. After the tractor with its front mower had driven past, I cut off several stalks with my sickle and cast them behind me; quickly, I moved on a metre and cleared away the next ones. At the end of my fifteen-metre strip the blades of several stalks had entwined. As I tore at them with the sickle to separate them, on the right-hand edge of the field I saw the tractor advance anew. I lost focus, my strength left me and my arm went limp. While I gave it a quick shake, the tractor trundled past again.

During lunch, whispers drifted over from the farm labourers' table. "The professor's daughter may be bright up top, but her arms are pretty useless."

Someone sniggered.

I turned red and lowered my head. When I left the dining hall I avoided everyone's gaze.

That evening I took a walk between the fields. The earth stuck to my shoes in thick clods. I walked so long through the darkness that my eyes almost shut as I went. As soon as I was in bed surrounded by sleeping girls, thoughts of that afternoon spun round my head once more. I switched on the table light I shared with the next girl and swivelled it towards the wall. Then I began to write a letter to my parents. I said I was exhausted, that I did not really fit in here, but mentioned nothing specific; afterwards, I tore the letter up.

I knew it stood within my father's power to protect me from other people's cruel remarks. He could easily find out who had made fun of me and ask them in for a word. After that, fear of reprimand would keep my mockers quiet.

But I did not want to ask my father for help, either in this or any other matter; if I got along without him, my pride would remain intact and I would be spared the farm labourers' resentment.

 co

In winter the earth turned hard. At around three o'clock in the morning I would stumble numbly over to the byre, hit the sleeping cows on their rumps with a stick and call them by name. Their bulky bodies felt warm to the touch. Along with a farm girl and one trainee, I fed the beasts before we mucked out the byre, scattered fresh straw and drove the cows to the milking parlour in the yard. As I hand-milked some sensitive cows, I would think of the sweet calves in the opposite stall, their soft lowing and their thirst; perhaps I could have a look in their stall afterwards. I would wish for the sun to be up when I left them, and that it would be a bright day.

After work, I was now in the habit of taking an evening stroll through the surrounding area. My eyes quickly grew accustomed to the faint light, so that each time I recognised the contours of the land better, easily discerned the paths, trees, meadows and fences. Shrouded in my coat and woollen scarf I was at one with the winter air, the dormant plants, the sleeping animals, on some days with the snow, luminous against the dark.

One evening, at the edge of a meadow I spotted a man's silhouette, static and slightly stooped, hands clasped behind his back. He turned to me as I approached.

"The evening air here," he said by way of greeting, "reminds me of home."

I recognised the young man's face; he too worked on the farm.

"Where are you from?" I asked, and he named a village near my boarding school. I told him where I had gone to school and how fondly I remembered my time there. He mumbled in surprise that no one else here knew his village.

We were silent for a moment; then he said, "I learned some of the work when I was a child: harvesting crops and milking goats."

I nodded, and was surprised to think that he had also noticed me on the farm.

"I'm here to deepen my knowledge before I start my studies," he continued, and proceeded to tell me that while it was still light on his early autumn walks he had picked plants at the field perimeters and set up a herbarium. "I don't mind the winter," he said.

I rubbed my hands together, formed two small hollows and breathed into them. We were not far from the farmyard when he offered me his gloves. I hesitated. Then my hands slipped into the already warm wool.

In the meagre light of the murky farmyard lantern, I noticed he had a slight squint in his left eye and blushed under my gaze. Although he did not come across as very athletic and looked poorly suited to hard farm work, I felt at ease in his presence, precisely because there was nothing boisterous or uncouth about the way he talked and behaved. As we said goodnight he asked me my name.

"Margret," I told him.

And he told me his – Hans – before adding, "The women in my village don't have as nice-sounding names as yours."

∞

Several years have passed since that evening stroll. Hans helped me to get through the year on the farm without me becoming completely isolated from the others.

During my final weeks on placement I often thought back to my schooldays and felt a desperate desire to read, to at last re-immerse myself in books. I scoured the little library next to the dining hall for books that had nothing to do with farming, and, sitting on the wooden bench at the farm entrance, I read works by Seghers and Borchert, Marx, Lessing, Büchner and Schiller. When trainees or farm labourers walked past I tried to ignore their comments. At the end of my placement I decided I wanted to be a German teacher.

Thereafter, I saw Hans every now and then at university and we exchanged a few words, until, this year past – it was a crisp, spring-like day at the end of February – we met while walking through the botanical gardens. We strolled side by side, as before. Hans explained the names of the trees and flowers and, when we left the gardens, picked me some daisies with pretty little petals from the grass. I thanked him with a quick kiss on the cheek, the way Rosa often used to brush my cheek with her lips when she passed.

Later we talked about the poems we liked, about our studies, the reasons we had both joined the Party[†] early on. Hans said we had a special duty to fulfil in our country, and I nodded. He walked me to my apartment (I had moved in at the start of my studies), awkwardly removed his glasses and kissed me under the protective cover of evening darkness. Even now, when I hug or kiss him by day, he blushes; and, although I have suggested it various times, Hans has yet to stay the night.

In two years he will have finished his studies and then, or perhaps even sooner, we want to marry and look for an apartment together, which we will adorn with flowers fresh and dried.

One day, shortly before my father's visit last year, I introduced Hans to my parents, but we stayed only an hour at most. At the time I still occasionally took the tram to my parents' house, suffered my father's silence and my mother's nagging, and attended to her for a few hours like a good husband should have. Each time, I was glad in one way when I arrived and glad in another when I left.

I showed Hans the garden, and we kissed next to the house wall where Rosa had often stood. For the first time in ages I saw squirrels scurry up tree trunks again and jump from tree to tree. Before setting off, we gathered hazelnuts under the old bush, like children. Hans found a bluish-black bird feather which he admired, attributed to a jay then carefully tucked away in his jacket pocket. Back at my apartment he laid it on my desk next to my little glass vase, and later, when sunlight sometimes slanted through the vase, the feather seemed to shimmer. The hazelnuts I ground in my coffee grinder and mixed through the dough which I baked into a cake for us. As always, Hans left in the evening, and I busied myself with a book for advanced-level pupils.

༄

I think the key thing today is to choose the right books for our pupils, books that spell out how they can shape our society. In those who rarely read we must also awaken an interest in the future our country aspires to as it distances itself from the past. Young people today still know poverty, but not war. Books have been written for them that speak of that, but also of the present and the future.

When I see pupils in front of me, some with bored faces, others from homes where the past is not spoken of, I worry about not reaching them with my message. What do I say to them when they enthuse about their relatives' fashionable clothes, the music that teenagers listen to on the other side of the Wall†? That they will enjoy the same advantages a few years hence if they help? Wealth means little to me. And what if there are no questions? I do not want to shout at people like my mother, who was also a teacher before the war.

Cat Dreams

Hans • 1967

Hans's mother called him at around ten in the evening: "The doctor said it'll soon be over." She sounded tired and deflated.

That night, Hans dreamed that his mother left his father sprawled on the floor with a head wound. In his dream, his father had watched television, as he did every evening, while his mother begrudgingly waited to carry him to bed. When his father clasped his arms around her neck so she could carry him on her back, she thought she would choke from his tight grip and vigorously shook her shoulders and head. Hans's father fell to the floor and cracked his skull on the oven while his mother, gasping for breath, hurried into the bedroom and double-locked the door.

Hans awoke with a racing heart, wiped the perspiration from his upper body with his pyjama top and washed in the sink of the small guesthouse room. He would put in a request for a few days' holiday; under the circumstances, the head of the herbarium would have to accept it.

∞

In the hospital ward Hans pressed the warm, calloused hand of his father, who seemed unchanged.

"I'll pop my clogs here, for sure," Hans heard him say, and thought that he would talk in exactly the same way if a doctor or nurse were present.

On a chair slightly away from the bed sat Hans's dozing mother, her head sunk on her bosom. The smells of disinfectant, coffee and floor polish failed to mask the smell of his mother's and father's sweat. Hans stood awkwardly by the bed because there was no second chair.

Suddenly a pained expression spread across his father's face; he screwed up his eyes and pressed his lips together. Hans grabbed him by the shoulder and turned him on his side. His father gently groaned. Hans reached for the button beside the bed, but his father gestured dismissively. "Leave it, lad, I don't need them. They'll only meddle with me."

After his mother had woken up, she and Hans took turns until evening so that one of them was always with his father to pass him a cup or help him eat, sit him up, lie him down again, exchange a few words from time to time, fetch him an extra blanket and remove it again if he became too warm.

As they left, Hans's mother promised she would visit again the following day.

When Hans nodded in affirmation, his father said, "Just you help your mother."

Hans and his mother did not talk on the bus home. Hans felt her warm, fleshy hips pressing against his own through the woollen fabric. His quickened breathing and the heat rising in his face bothered him, but the bus being full meant he could not edge away from her to stretch his leg or he would block the aisle.

At home his mother prepared a quick supper of goat's cheese, liverwurst and bread from the *Konsum*†. Hans remembered an evening with Margret's parents when he had been surprised to discover that

18

there was such good food in the city, and Margret's mother had told him, not without pride, about a shop that sold exclusively to university staff and their relatives. Usually Hans loved the taste of his mother's food, but tonight he had as little appetite as she. The silence in the house spoke of his father.

After supper his mother offered to let him sleep beside her on his father's mattress because the top floor was not heated. Hans knew how cold it could be up there in October. Around midnight he climbed the stairs, draped a blanket over the window, took a pair of his old pyjamas from the wardrobe and with a shiver buried himself under the clammy feather duvet.

After breakfast the next morning, his mother went to see his father. Hans accompanied her into the garden. The path from the shed to the front door was partly laid with stone slabs, which had not been the case on Hans's last visit. Where the slabs ended, a shallow trench ran to the shed.

"Your father did it all," his mother said. "Even cast the slabs. Lay and supported his whole body on his arms and slid forwards. Sometimes had sore knees afterwards but carried on next day. Feels nothing in his legs, anyway." Hans was amazed how neatly the slabs fitted. He would struggle to work as meticulously.

In the shed he found a wheelbarrow and loaded it with slabs. As soon as he lifted the barrow off the ground the weight dragged on his arms and shoulders. On the farm placement they had had to hump baskets of potatoes over to a trailer. In the ensuing years Hans had not worked physically but instead taken part in field trips, written reports, created herbaria, made lecture notes. The barrow wobbled as he wheeled it over the doorsill of the small wooden hut, looking down while trying to keep the barrow steady. The mild pain above his shoulder blades would last no more than a minute.

Suddenly their cat leapt towards him. Hans had missed her the night before. She regularly roamed the village and hissed at people; only in Hans's presence did she purr. Hans stopped in fright, making the barrow tip and several slabs slide out, one of which broke under the weight of the others.

"Cats bring bad luck," his mother usually said. "Trample the flowerbeds, ruin the vegetables. Mostly it's black ones."

Perhaps she was right. For all that Hans had missed the cat the previous night, now he vehemently shook the leg she was rubbing against. He had never been entirely at ease with her, even though he enjoyed her affection. His father liked to annoy her by tugging her ears or tail, pretending to quietly bark or setting a dog on her.

For years as a child, night after night Hans had dreamed of jet-black, sparkly-eyed cats that suddenly morphed into black-haired witches. The witches uttered curses. If they appeared in the last six days of the old year or the first six days of the new, their curses would come true, his mother had said. Even though the curses had remained benign until now, one day they might not, and not only at the turn of the year. To this day, on those twelve winter nights Hans endeavoured to get by without sleep. Every year, after his first night awake, his eyes would begin to droop, and sleep would overcome him either on the sofa, during breakfast or lunch at his parents' place (whom he visited over Christmas), or on a shop floor after he had lain down exhausted in a quiet corner. The dreams, though, did not disappear.

Luckily Hans could not remember a single dream from last night. Before falling asleep it had not even occurred to him that he might have "one of those dreams".

Silently the cat slunk around his right leg. Hans gave her a sharp kick, but when she meowed he lifted her up and laid his head against her fur. My mother can go to the devil with her proverbs, he thought, and was appalled at himself. Putting the cat back down, he dragged the broken slab back to the shed and began work.

In the early evening, when Hans's mother returned from the city, plodded down from the garden gate across the lawn (avoiding the trench) and stopped beside him, he was wearing only tracksuit bottoms and vest, and beads of sweat dripped from his face.

"You'll catch cold," she cautioned him, but Hans hardly heard her. He had needed eight hours to first level the earth, free it of stones, spread sand and then lay each of the four slabs. More than once he had had to readjust them, displacing the sand below

His mother told him that his father was a little better, even though the doctors refused to believe it. Hans replied that *he* believed it because his father did not give up so easily; sometimes you could even forget he was ill.

His mother looked at him in bemusement. "I'll go chop wood," she responded.

৪৩

During the night the duvet glimmered white. Hans glanced at the wallpaper on the sloping ceiling across which scampered black cats. He thought of Margret, her blonde hair, and felt himself grow hard. He touched himself, but instantly withdrew his hand. The black cats screeched and made him shiver. His heart rate increased; at the same time, the warmth seemed slowly to drain from his body. In his mind's eye he saw a photo of his mother in a black dress, very young, sitting on the armrest of a chair, hands folded on her lap, a silver cross round her neck, smiling through thin lips. Behind her his father was standing in a suit. His father's right arm was only partly visible, so his right hand must have been resting either on his mother's back or that of the chair. Hans was standing in front of his father in a white

21

polo-neck sweater and white knitted knee socks, with his side parting combed flat.

The minister said you did not touch yourself. His mother said you did not touch yourself. His father said nothing.

Freezing, Hans got up, padded downstairs, pausing outside the door to his parents' room before going down to the cellar. As he shovelled coal into the metal bucket he heard the thud of footsteps on the stairs. His mother's ample bosom and soft stomach showed beneath her nightgown. She looked at him, strangely awake.

"Coal's expensive," she said, before her eyes strayed from the coal bucket to Hans's pyjama bottoms.

From then on, she did not offer to let him sleep next to her, even though night by night it turned colder. In Hans's dreams, witches and creatures swirled around and chased him, but never caught him. One night he awoke in the early hours and, hearing his mother bustling below in the kitchen, would have liked to hurry down to her to be comforted.

∞

A few days later, Hans pushed his father's three-wheeled buggy over to the bus stop and rolled it to the bus door as his mother got out with his father on her back. Hans grabbed him under the armpits, and together they seated him in the buggy, which he drove by himself.

"They can't keep me down," laughed his father.

Hans and his mother fed the fan belt round the drive shaft on the side of the buggy and then stood back. His father gave the leather belt a firm backwards tug. Today he managed to start the motor first time. As he drove, he waved, now right, now left, to the villagers who drew aside their curtains and stared. Hans wondered whether the people in the village, when not at work, waited as much as they used to for people to walk or drive by; whether the noise of the approaching buggy drew them to the window by habit, or because they wanted to make sure that their contribution towards the vehicle had been worthwhile.

As his father steered the buggy over the lawn past the unfinished pathway, he said quietly to Hans, "Leave the slabs for me, please."

Taken aback, Hans looked at the slabs he had laid and could hardly spot the difference between his own work and that of his father. Because his father seemed to show neither displeasure nor reproach, Hans suspected that he had meant something else: feeding and killing the animals, cutting the grass, chopping the wood and stacking it in the attic – there were the things his father could not do.

Inside the house, Hans and his mother lifted his father out of the buggy and put him on a chair; his father braced himself against the backrest and slid forwards while his mother depressed the seat. Hans went back out to the garden. Weeks ago his mother had scythed the grass, turned it, left it to dry then piled it in the attic space above the top room. The remaining stubble looked like bristles.

∞

Hans tried to picture his mother before the war, when his father still had good legs and he was yet to be born.

After Hans's father returned from captivity as a prisoner of war, his mother took Hans with her every day to his grandfather's farm, or else his field, a compact area of ground close to the farm. Hans's grandfather was a foreman at the ore kilns and rarely home. At the farm, Hans's mother met with her sisters, whose children already attended school. Hans would pet the rabbits' thin, soft fur, make patterns from grass blades, or from a low wall watch the brown hens greedily peck the thinly scattered grains. He often felt hungry and would nibble on dandelion leaves.

Once he started school, Hans and his mother worked on the farm for several months, while day after day his father continued to go to the glassworks in the next village. Hans bit into the raw potatoes he picked, and his mother would snatch them from his mouth. She also forbade him to beg at the *Konsum*. With hands reddened from work she showed him how to milk the goat, guiding his hands onto the udder. She cooked tasty meals from potatoes, butter and milk, and let Hans watch the animals being killed, to teach him how to do it. She sent him with other boys to tend the goat on the big meadow, but little did she know that no sooner had one of the boys launched the rubber ball they had brought along to play headers with, Hans simply tethered it. Later his mother showed him how to cut grass in their own garden, but only rarely was Hans able to swish the scythe as swiftly and surely as she; he always left one or two blades standing, and these he patiently pulled out until the lawn looked even.

On Sundays, the three of them went to the little slate church on the hill at the edge of the village.

"We need to go so there's rabbit and dumplings afterwards," his father once whispered with a gentle laugh. Later he said, "You two go without me – my buggy takes up the space of three devout people."

As soon as Hans sat down next to his mother on the hard wooden pew, she spread a woollen blanket over their knees. All the same, Hans shivered, even in summer, as the minister's sonorous voice echoed in the dim building. The stories he told from the pulpit sounded like olden fairy tales. Usually Hans's mother retold them before bed; even though she simplified them, they remained stories about bad people who were punished and good people who were rewarded. The greater the suffering they underwent, the greater the recognition they enjoyed afterwards. His mother made it sound as though the men and women she told of could have dwelled in their midst. These stories resonated with Hans long afterwards, and he hardly ever failed to forget his mother's penetrating gaze, or that of the minister.

After Hans's confirmation, the minister took him aside and asked, "Could you see yourself being a minister?" Hans was perplexed and for several days did not speak to anyone about it; then he called on the minister to tell him no.

"Why not?" asked the minister in his faintly nasal voice. He took Hans by the arm and turned him to face the pulpit. "The people will listen to you, and you'll earn good money. Even here in this country."

"There are other jobs just as necessary," Hans said evasively

The following year Hans was one of the first in the village to celebrate *Jugendweihe*†, at which point the minister forbade him ever to enter the church again.

෮

From the garden gate Hans gazed over at the patches of lumpy earth where potatoes and turnips would grow again in the coming year. Beside both brown beds, dark-red and yellow chrysanthemums were in bloom; beyond, Hans saw the three small redcurrant bushes whose fruit he had picked in cups, pots and jars over countless summers. Strange that his mother should have been the first to suggest he go away to the city. Sometimes Hans had actually felt drawn elsewhere; nowhere in particular – but would he of his own accord have left the woods, this garden, the animals, this house? His mother had said that, as he got on so well at school, he must attend secondary school and study afterwards; perhaps then one day he would return with his wife – doctors and engineers were needed in the village, too. His father agreed: he had the makings of a scholar.

Slowly Hans walked back to the door. In the living-room-cum-kitchen his mother was preparing supper with a serious face, while his father darned one of her socks and whistled to himself. Hans shut the kitchen door behind him and climbed the creaking stairs to the attic space. On the floor lay hay like the hair trimmings of some strange creature. As he lifted a sheaf, the chimney at the far end caught his eye. Often in his nightly dreams a blaze broke out – started by hay heaped up against the chimney stack – and spread throughout the house, the family's sole possession. Hurriedly Hans closed the hatch. Back downstairs he opened the first rabbit hutch and put food in the far corner of the tiny grilled box, so the rabbit did not jump out. Once busy eating, it would not mind the restricted space any more than the other rabbits, which Hans fed one by one. Sooner or later they would all be killed anyway.

A white bowl of potato dumplings was steaming on the kitchen table. The smell of rabbit meat filled the room. Hans's eyes rested on the little wall calendar above the sofa, which featured well-known lines from an old poem: *Far more flowers while you live / for they're no use on the grave**. Today was Thursday. Even though he could hardly eat a thing, he was grateful to his mother for the meal when he saw the enormous relish with which his father ate and how he praised the food, complimented his mother, talked about hospital and laughed. A few days ago the silence had robbed Hans of his appetite. Now his father's laughter filled the kitchen. Even the house spoke to Hans in uncanny, long-forgotten voices.

His mother got up first, went over to the kitchen sideboard and swivelled out the washing-up surface with its two enamel basins. She filled the kettle, reached for the matches and, when the kettle whistled a few minutes later, poured cold water into the left-hand basin and added hot. Then she gripped the back of his father's seat, beckoned to Hans, and together they pushed his father over to the basins. His father placed a plate coated in soapsuds in the right-hand basin, and Hans picked it up and wiped it dry with the dishtowel.

Later his father watched television lying on the sofa. His mother rested for a moment at the dinner table, and Hans sat with her. When she got up again, Hans asked if she had heard from the boys he used to tend the goat with.

"They still live in the village," his mother replied, and pointed either way with her arms. "One works up front at the factory, the other at the *LPG†*." As though she had read Hans's thoughts she added, "They both have young children. You can't go round now." And as she wiped the hob with a cloth, she cast Hans a sideways glance and asked casually, "Nothing on the cards yet for you two?"

Hans reddened and shook his head. He asked his mother to call him when his father wished to go to bed; or else his father could call him, so that she need not stay up. As Hans slipped through the door to go up to the attic space, his mother whispered that she would have liked more children.

Hans had not discussed children with Margret. No doubt one day they would come. Sometimes Margret pushed him away; she must have her days then – or fear getting pregnant. Hans did not know what the right words were; he preferred to respect her wish not to couple with him. On their wedding night, when he had seen her naked for the first time, he would willingly have fled the scene. They had not made love; instead, Margret had covered him up and nuzzled into his shoulders until his trembling stopped. Despite numerous attempts, it was weeks before they consummated the marriage; after that, it took a long time till Margret – now it was she who trembled – was open to him again.

Hans got to his feet when his mother called. Downstairs he was met by the welcoming warmth of the living-room-cum-kitchen. His mother helped his father sit up as Hans dragged a chair over to the sofa, sat on it and arched his back. After his father had clasped his arms around Hans's neck, Hans stood up and carried him through to the turned-down bed. Once lying there, gazing at the ceiling, his father never forgot to say thank you. His wasted legs looked grey against the white sheet. Hans tucked him in and wished him goodnight before his mother shut the bedroom door behind her, as though with her last energy of the day.

ಐ

Despite the poor soundproofing, it was ten minutes before his father's rasping snores reached Hans. He decided that at daybreak, before leaving for the city, he would stand in the wide meadow where the goat had once grazed and he had played headers with the boys, and feel the wind at his back, ruffling his hair. He would like to walk one day with Margret down the gentle slope over to the wood, to the mosses, streams and fallen branches, as they had once walked together on the farm. He thought of the grubby yellow rubber ball flying through the air, his mother standing on the narrow street calling him back to his grandfather's house, the white goat bleating as it trotted at his side; his father, who sat at home more and more because his legs no longer obeyed him; and lastly, on the far side of the wood, Hans thought to make out a cat-like creature of indeterminate colour, shadowy and indistinct.

Armoured Protection

Friedrich • 1968

The air coming through my study window is still chilly. From the garden I think I detect the fragrance of sour cherries, which Marie will pick in the coming days, a faint scent in contrast to the vitreous red of the cherries in the morning light.

I turn the radio dial; the speaker's soft voice grows louder. Though it is only eight o'clock, the telephone has already rung several times. I am advised that I should be prepared for possible unrest at the university and should note the names of students with deviant views.

I needn't prepare for my lecture; I know what I will say, even if a student asks an unexpected question. All these victories would not have been wrought without the Soviet Army. We should not deride or berate the Soviets, as is fashionable just now in the West; rather, we should place our trust in them. How can the West compare the present situation with that of the past – as though they foresee a war – without speaking of guilt, of justice? How can they equate fascism's inhumane ideology with the concept of delivering human beings from human exploitation?

The road to communism is long and rocky – anyone who still belongs to us today knows that. But was not the October Revolution – the victory of the proletariat, of people hungering for justice over the aristocrats – was not this victory, upon which socialism was founded, immeasurably harder? And has the fight against fascism not demanded from us the utmost in terms of courage and sacrifice, mental and physical strength?

∞

Back then, just after Hitler came to power, I already foresaw and feared the outbreak of war. For that reason I set off for Prague, to write my dissertation there. How often have people started to dread another war, barely has one ended? Now it is on their minds again, whereas the real danger emanates not from the tanks in Wenceslas Square but from the relentless armament of Western nations. For years I have spoken and written against the tenet that it might be in the interest of socialist nations to build more nuclear weapons, because it altogether contradicts what we have lived through, as well as the basic communist principle. The oppressed should have the right to a life free from hunger and dependency – how can that be reconciled with the horrors of war? With humanity's total annihilation?

What the fascists did to the Soviet people obligates us to support the Soviets unconditionally. To this day I am ashamed because I served in the *Wehrmacht*† until the end of the war. Yes, in the years leading up to the outbreak of war the fascists managed to silence me too.

I never did learn how they found us. In any case, after we had hidden the stationery, typewriter and duplicator above the attic hatch, and two of my comrades had calmly opened the door, there they were, already waving one of our pamphlets. Seconds later I could hardly move my hands. I felt my eardrums throb to their yells. Only once I lay in the cell did I slowly begin to hear again. Later I often wished I had been deaf, when their voices ricocheted off the walls between interrogations: the tall, black-haired man's piercing voice, which at first sounded soft and mellow then developed a sharp edge, giving off cracks like gunfire until finally, venting his apparent fury, it blasted right next to my ear so that my head threatened to burst; others chose a more confusing sequence. At night I tried to analyse their methods, and this gave me the feeling of being strong despite my weak physical state – but only for so long, until in the next room they made Rosa or another baby cry. They didn't show me the infant. Had they realised the state I was in, there and then they could have extracted the names of comrades I was friendly with.

A few days later my uncle paid for my release and hammered home to me the need to keep quiet in future, to not stand out, nor refuse if I was drafted.

He never told me with whom he had made a deal or how much he had paid.

At the front I didn't tell anyone I had been in prison. But afterwards, during my captivity as a prisoner of war, I showed the English the grubby, tattered papers detailing my first time in prison. Shortly thereafter two soldiers drove me and one other prisoner to Hamburg. Meagre trees grew amid the debris of bombed buildings. The military vehicle stopped in front of a tall, undestroyed house. The soldiers handed us our release papers and handed me over to two administrators, who led me into a small room on the ground floor that had been made into an office with two tables, two chairs and some lockers. They invited me to sit at a table with names, swastikas and German sayings carved into it. The man who explained to me how to dispense ration cards shrugged: "There aren't any other desks."

I asked if he couldn't at least cover it with something, but then we both looked around the room and gazed out of the dull window pane at the people stumbling over rubble. When our eyes met I waved the matter aside.

I felt sorry for the people and their children who came to me from then on. You saw the hunger in their faces. Some of the children asked me if I had a sweet or a little sugar for them, and their mothers placated them with the promise of bread and butter that evening. Far behind me on the other side of the square, women with little picks prized slates from the ruins and passed them from hand to hand. In the time I worked there, three house-like structures arose in this way. Men I saw but rarely. Each day, I asked myself where the women got their strength from and where their children were playing at that moment. Sometimes the women came over to me, shrouded in dust: their faces and arms were constantly coated in a thin dusty layer. When they entered they pulled off their gloves, and I saw the wounds on their fingers and palms.

Many stooped as they shuffled past the office window. Only after they had entered did they straighten up. Only children would push open the door with both hands and come running in.

∞

Nine months later my children charged into the room. I didn't recognise them. Margret, the blonde tomboy, I was seeing for the first time; Tanya was far thinner than I remembered; Rosa, who walked behind her sisters as if on stilts, could have been Margret's young mother. Rosa's face vaguely reminded me of someone I knew. Only my wife Johanna, walking slowly behind them, did I instantly recognise. She had aged years.

All at once Johanna sat down on the stone floor and broke into sobs. She was so skeletal that I removed my jacket and placed it under her. Rosa, almost as thin, came over and wavered for a moment in front of me before pressing herself to my stomach. Meanwhile the other two girls played catch.

"Is that all the luggage you have?" I asked, indicating the bulging kitbag and the small suitcase beside it.

Johanna nodded.

"And where will you stay?"

"A small place near Bremen," she replied. "We're registered there."

"The Englanders have allocated me a room in a young family's apartment," I told her and explained that the wife there was still waiting for her husband to return from captivity.

After work I shouldered the kitbag and took Tanya and Margret by the hand. Johanna and Rosa got to their feet with a slight swing. In the administration office hall, hundreds of other refugees were sitting around. Several hours later, when we were asked in to one of the rooms, the city lay shrouded in a strange, rural darkness broken only by the occasional searchlight or lantern. Rosa jumped down from the windowsill where she had been silently watching the people. Tanya and Margret said goodbye to a girl they had been playing with. The girl held aloft her woollen doll's ragged yellow hand and waved it back and forth in goodbye.

The man I spoke to, and whom I tried to make understand that Johanna deserved the same preferential treatment as I, shook his head: where possible, families had already taken in refugees, he said. I lent my words a forceful edge, as impatiently he looked to the door. When Johanna interrupted us, I noted that her English was just as good as before. But the man again shook his head regretfully. Johanna clasped my shirt before suddenly, soundlessly, collapsing onto the floor. Rosa immediately bent over her. The man hurried to find me the address of a doctor and a nearby refugee camp. Quickly he wrote out the necessary papers for Johanna and the children, so that they could move closer to me.

Below on the street a couple of men were standing in front of a car, trading cigarettes. I asked if one of them could drive us to the camp at the edge of town, but they promptly climbed into their car.

Johanna, supported by Rosa, pleaded that I put her and the children up for the night. I told her that by doing so I risked losing my own room. Eventually a military vehicle stopped in front of the building, and I persuaded the driver to take us with him. We drove past ruins, solitary figures scurrying through them in the fading light, until the streets deteriorated into sandy tracks lined intermittently with huts. Sand billowed up when the driver braked. I made out rows of narrow barracks with window frames that glowed brightly. Around midnight I walked home alone.

I visited Johanna and the girls every day. Trudged over rain-softened earth to the decaying wooden barracks, said a polite hello to the other families and sat down on one of two steel-framed beds my family had been allocated. Everyone lived alongside one another in quiet respect, whispered where possible, urged children not to run around, or only outside. The walls were blackened with mildew and grime. When the sun shone I wandered around the grounds with the children and we collected stones, wood and grass to play with. One day, I brought Johanna a washing basin (a present from the family I lived with) so that she no longer had to wash clothes in her tiny little cooking pot. Later I saw to their ration cards. Always before I left to go back to my room, Johanna hugged me as though she doubted I would return. Whereas she hugged me harder and longer by the day, her energy for everyday existence seemed steadily to diminish; she found it hard just to stand up, and she moved like an old woman.

After a few weeks Johanna said to me, "I think it's better if we send the children to a home, just temporarily; perhaps they'll be better fed there and given some clothes." She told me she had already made inquiries and found out about a home near Hamburg run by the Swiss Red Cross. The building was undamaged, and they took children for a modest fee.

Although appalled at the idea of sending the children away so soon after their return, I didn't oppose her; besides, my money barely sufficed to pay the rent at the barracks. When I made to leave the camp that day, Margret gripped my trouser legs and screamed. She held on with such strength and determination that I couldn't quietly loosen her grip. Directly next to the children an old man stirred from his sleep and sat up. Brusquely he grabbed Margret's upper arm and glowered at her. "If you're not quiet, I'll lock you in there," he said, and pointed to a small, worn leather suitcase. Margret's screams turned to frightened sobs. Briefly I pressed her to me and left.

The next day I packed some supplies in a bag, went to the camp, explained the trains to Rosa, handed her a piece of paper with the address of the home, urged her to keep a close eye on the children, and, if they should be delayed, to look for a safe place for the night. Rosa nodded faintly, no tears, no complaint. Johanna and I promised the children we would come and fetch them soon. The two little ones scuttled behind Rosa and didn't turn round.

I visited Johanna every day after work as before. She spoke little, mentioned only that she slept fitfully in the midst of the strange people. I didn't tell her that almost every night I dreamed of being chased for kilometres before finally being shot, that the moment the shot was fired I woke up, deaf to all other noise save the gunshot bang and my own screams. I dreamed of Johanna being shot, Rosa, Tanya and Margret; I dreamed of mutilated corpses, and blood that fell from the sky instead of rain, and when I woke up bathed in sweat, I was glad I could get up and go to work.

∞

Several months passed before I applied for a lectureship in philosophical materialism at a university in Thuringia. I was given the position in the winter semester. They wrote that the university would see to an entry permit for the East Zone†. Johanna wrote a letter to the children and one to the director of the home, asking her to send the children back by the safest route possible. When the director let us know the children's expected day of arrival, I handed over my duties to the other staff at the office and hurried to the train station with Johanna. It was a warm, bright day in early autumn. I didn't know whether Johanna (who clung to me on the way, leaned on me all the more as we neared the station) was looking forward to seeing the children; her expression remained surprisingly unconcerned.

The children didn't alight from any of the arriving carriages. Johanna said that most likely there had been disruptions, as often occurred, but I ran up and down the platform and asked if anyone had heard news of our children, or of a train crash.

They came the following morning on a train from the north, the three of them – as I saw at once with relief – and looked healthier and stronger than when they had left. Johanna and I had spent the night in the station. Tanya and Margret looked at not only me but also Johanna as though we were people they had once known long ago, whereas Rosa simply told us they had mixed up their trains. She remained rigid when I hugged her. We told the children we would soon be able to move into an apartment together, but none of them responded.

ଚ୨

How the city must have changed! I mean Prague, with its wonderful lanes and bridges, its unique history. How well the people will now be faring in their warm apartments, in newly built, unostentatious buildings that perhaps look a little odd next to the houses from the turn of the century. But beauty is something we will think about as soon as no one needs to watch their pennies anymore.

What a tiny room I lived in as a student lodger – while the house owners, with two floors at their disposal, would nightly invite people to dinner in their high, cavernous rooms. On the city map I see the house fell victim to bomb attacks.

I do not see what has driven the people in Prague onto the streets; why they aren't prepared to make sacrifices; why they don't understand that you get nothing for free; that it's true the hardest years are behind us, but that we run right into the enemy's arms if we lose sight of the goal; that the freedom they desire is only something for self-seekers and is at the end of the day still subject to the law of the survival of the fittest.

Naturally we need to discuss with each other and listen to dissenting views, but does everyone really have to publicly proclaim whatever comes into their heads in moments of lucidity or confusion, deep despondency or utter elation, unpredictable rage or unconditional forbearance towards their fellow human beings – during any mood swings whatsoever?

Over a decade ago, I felt personally the harmful effects of such an open atmosphere when a West German high-school group invited me to give a lecture on historical materialism. There were only young people in the lecture theatre, impassioned and insistent, as is characteristic of the younger generation, asking questions about the 17th of June Uprising[†], which, to be honest, placed me in a quandary. I had a duty to perform – thus aggrieved, should I have asked myself why I had been invited? On the way home I was glad to be out of the firing line of their questions, but I could easily have ended up like other philosophers who acted carelessly and less loyally. Of course I was repulsed by the arrest of colleagues, whom I knew as communists and antifascists, but I also had to ask myself why they had run this risk and not tempered their criticism. Were they really still on our side?

After the trip I was seized by anxiety. Every morning I went to my lectures and told the tried and tested, things I was certain I wouldn't be liable for. At the same time I sensed some students' unrest, their disappointment that I never once encouraged a discussion concerning current events in our country, either directly or in a passing allusion. Several times after a lecture I heard a small section of the student body discuss in whispers why my lectures lacked passion. When I realised I simply had to change something, from one day to the next I included, as a shining reminder of my lecture in the West, a recent book by a West German sociologist about the scepticism of the younger generation.

Soon I realised something wasn't right. My mind was in terrible disarray. As I spoke to the students I felt ashamed because I believed I had betrayed my convictions. The directionless nature of my thoughts, which changed week on week, seemed to rip me asunder. As a result, at the end of the semester in the final exam it was unfeasible to demand of the students knowledge I had not imparted to them. I was invited in for a chat with the university party leadership. What was I supposed to say? I admitted everything, took all the blame – visions of my prison cell and the interrogations pursuing me like a ravenous beast.

∞

How could I have explained that to Margret as I sat on the narrow stool in her kitchen and spotted the gleam in her eyes which she sought to hide?

On that day in the lecture theatre, I had been angry that she had dragged a private matter into the public sphere, angry because I couldn't afford any further loss of stability. That she would be unable to sever all ties with me: these words of hers had moved me in a curious way. Furthermore, I was irritated beyond measure that there before me stood a young woman, confident and tall, whose development I had missed out on. Need I reproach myself for anything? Years of hard work lie behind me, during which I have honed and shaped my worldview, worked through doubt and uncertainty, and played my part in building a country, whose founding was a matter of concern to me and whose preservation is now.

In every era, children have grown up alongside their parents and nursemaids, played or worked, had sufficient to eat or else stolen, left their parents of their own free will or out of necessity. I do what is possible to form a place where children are welcome.

Such places should not be jeopardised. The tanks show us the right road. They will only shoot as a last resort, and only arrest those whose intention is to hinder us in the formation of a humane and kindly existence.

Waiting for Friedrich

Johanna • 1971

Margret, do you know I was pregnant once before Rosa? That I was married to another man? When I started to vomit more than twice a day, I called on a midwife I was friendly with, whose husband, a surgeon, removed the foetus on their kitchen table. Only to start with did I notice the hardness of the table, just as many women hardly feel the pain of the stitches after giving birth. I knew women could bleed this heavily but had never witnessed it. Even so, the sight of the sheets and hand towels stained red after the operation affected me little.

But I looked forward to having Rosa because I loved your father as much as I do today. We met in Wrocław† – other people say Breslau – and lived together for a time in a tiny attic apartment. Round the house ran a little garden where in summer we welcomed relatives and friends. They would always bring something: meat or fresh bread, cake, fruit from their gardens, ruby-red and honey-golden wine. Your father was still studying; I taught at a primary school and earned our money from that. Then he went to Prague to write his dissertation, and I was pregnant without knowing it.

It was a good time for those who shut their eyes to what was coming. What if I had known that for years I would only get to see your father for a day at a time, while he was imprisoned? I needed Rosa to remind me of him, to feel him near me. Rosa and I slept in one bed until your father returned from the war; you and Tanya always slept in another. I only had milk for you for three weeks, Margret. After your feed, once the pain eased in my breast and your face turned dreamier, your lips softer and less ravenous, I placed a rag end in your mouth and put you down on the other bed; later, where there was just room for a blanket; and then, when we only had one bed, at the edge beside Rosa, where Tanya slept. I couldn't have tolerated the smell of someone else between Rosa and me.

No, you were not planned, but bearing you was my form of protest against the war. You were also my shield when the Soviet soldiers captured Wrocław and wreaked their revenge. Every time a soldier spoke to me I put my right arm around Rosa and my left around you and Tanya, and the longer he eyed me, the tighter I held you, trembling. Do you remember? No? To this day, your father thinks my fear was unnecessary.

Tanya was four, you two, when the fortress period began. For weeks we had known about the Red Army's advance. How insane must the German Army have been to declare a virtually besieged city a fortress and plunge its people into uncertainty? I refused to leave Wrocław. In any case I struggled to get you through the winter without serious illness. Later, at the roadsides we found the corpses of small children and old people. They had either frozen or starved to death.

I tried to carry on as usual and lead a normal everyday life with the three of you. From time to time I asked myself if we shouldn't have fled, particularly on nights when planes droned incessantly over the roofs. Then I would get out of bed and gaze at the city sky red with fire over other neighbourhoods. You and Tanya, you mostly slept through until morning, but I had to spend hours comforting Rosa to the sound of nearby rumbling and distant booming. I collected myself, insofar as

I could, and in the morning, after I had given Rosa all the necessary instructions and smiled reassuringly to you, I walked and walked through the streets of a city being bombed more each day. House walls, blackened, windowless, seemed to peer out at people from so many square eyes; the air reeked of smoke and the streets were strewn with glass shards, building debris and charred trees.

I bought food, visited relatives and invited them to our house, spoke with women who were tracing young men bearing a resemblance to members of their families, or else had, I presumed, sons of conscription age. I advised them to hide their sons and nephews to save them from perishing in battle. Some women began to cry; others gave the impression that they had already decided the same thing long ago and were simply waiting for someone to confirm they had been correct. One woman shouted that she would report me to the local Nazi leader, that incitement to desertion now warranted the death penalty. Waving aside her threat, I turned silently away, whereupon she shouted after me that she was proud of her son.

Every day I met groups of people walking over rubble, pulling behind them handcarts with the few belongings that the German soldiers had not set fire to in the street: carefully folded garments, silverware, photo albums. Now and then on the street I saw a ragged corpse, someone with no relatives; or else their family had not yet found them. Despite the approaching planes, many evacuees barely even lifted their heads. I, on the other hand, would hurry back to you if I found myself near our apartment. Almost invariably the three of you were already sitting in the air-raid shelter. Occasionally you cried, Margret.

I remember one bombing most clearly. I had just come through the door when I heard a plane circling directly above our neighbourhood and called your names in alarm. Rosa grabbed Tanya by the hand and hurriedly stumbled down the stairs after me. We forgot that half an hour earlier Rosa had laid you on our bed for your nap. Just after we got to the cellar a bomb struck our neighbourhood and made our house shake. Rosa jumped up first and, before I could restrain her, shoved her skinny body with all her might against the cellar door. Once she had opened it, she ran upstairs. You had woken up, tumbled onto the stairs and were clinging to the banister, bawling. But it was weeks later that Rosa told me this. She must have snatched you up at once because you made it to the cellar before the next bomb attack.

Our house remained unaffected until the end of the war. One by one we took in evacuated relatives and other people whose houses had been destroyed by bombs. Tante Anna – who got you up each morning, Margret, washed and dressed you, played "Bumpety Bump, Rider" with you and tossed you in the air – was discovered one March morning in a neighbour's attic. Two days previously, she had carried her fatally wounded daughter from the new airfield they were building, through the inner city to our house. When I opened the door to her, she wore an expression that haunted my dreams for a long time afterwards and caused me to get up in the middle of the night to make sure you were all right. Tante Anna stood bowed before me, her shoulders sagging from the weight of her child. But when I silently offered my help, she wouldn't let me take her daughter; she laid the girl on the blanket I spread out on the bed and tried all she could to resuscitate her.

The next morning, as it was getting light, Tante Anna went into the garden, searched for a bare spot and began to clear away earth with a tin dustpan. I didn't leave the house that day. On her knees she dug with no regard for her dress. We had spread a shawl over the girl and forbade any of you to go near. From the window Tante Anna's thin figure seemed to cave in more by the hour. The rests she took lasted longer each time. I was extremely glad that, as a mother of small children, I was exempt from labour duty – night and day thousands of women and young people were helping to build the runway for the German airplanes that were continually being shot down. Around lunchtime Tante Anna came up to us. She looked very pale and told us she was going to look for a bigger shovel, that the grave was still too narrow. The following day the neighbour rang our door and begged me to untie the rope from her attic ceiling.

We buried Tante Anna in our garden together with her thirteen-year-old daughter. During the burial, Oma Otillie stayed with you three in the apartment.

A short time afterwards, at Easter, the first snowdrops emerged next to the grave. I gazed at the thick, virtually black branches of the cherry tree and their bursting buds. Soon a cloud of white blossom would brighten the garden.

We urgently needed shoes for you and Tanya, so Opa Jakob offered to go into town to swap some jars of apple jelly for leather or some other strong material. Opa Jakob walked nimbly and quickly. His war wounds, the gravity of which he had enlarged to the authorities so as to qualify as disabled, had virtually healed. Even though he limped, only Rosa could keep up with him.

He had been away for several hours when a strange storm arose. For weeks, new houses were either ravaged by fire or collapsed in a blaze every day. We were used to the orange-red glow over the city, but this storm drove fire throughout entire neighbourhoods. Oma Ottilie came away from the window, said she felt ill and asked where Jakob had got to.

"Just feel my pulse," she said.

I shooed away Tanya, who wanted to sit on Oma Ottilie's lap. Rosa stood motionless by the window until I told her to play with you two. While I took Oma Ottilie to the bathroom I heard Rosa saying, "The doll will get pretty shoes too, yes, of... of snow, then they won't burn,

45

and with flowers on that shine so, yes…"

Hardly had I shut the bathroom door than Oma Ottilie collapsed. When Opa Jakob came back half an hour later – out of breath, face smudged with smoke, clutching a little wooden horse instead of a strip of leather – she was no longer alive.

Opa Jakob wept soundlessly. After Oma's death, he spoke little. Some days he would suddenly look up at me and talk half-vacantly about Friedrich. I listened to every word.

"If only there were post," was how Opa usually closed his stories. One time he said softly, "Our child," and I couldn't help but think of the many fathers who instead would have said, "My son."

I had little occasion to miss Friedrich. My days were filled, and at night I abandoned myself to a few hours' sleep when no planes were to be heard. Anyway, I could do as little for him as he could for me. When I thought of your father, I remembered our earlier time together. Although I could scarcely imagine a shared family life with him, I still hoped to see him again, one of the few inward emotions I was capable of until the end of the fortress period. Increasingly, even my fear gave way to indifference. We spent the final weeks almost continuously in the air-raid shelter. Whenever a bomb struck nearby most people prayed, some screamed. I knew that neither one nor the other would be heard. Even the terror in each of your eyes only triggered automatic reactions in me: take you in my arms, whisper words of comfort, press your heads to my breast, shut your ears with my hands until the shaking and shuddering, rumbling and booming was over; hold damp cloths to your faces when dust cascaded from the ceiling. Rosa held you tight, I held Tanya. Why not the other way around? I don't know; probably because you were the smallest, or because Rosa loved you more. Would I have carried you, Margret, if Rosa had not already been ten years old? Perhaps not.

Incidentally, Opa Jakob stayed with the Soviet soldiers, for whom he repaired shoes. They didn't pay him, but curiously he was allowed to stay on in our house. I didn't manage to visit him again before his death.

I might have personally placed you three and me on the lists for the *trek*† – but one of the Polish commanders decided at the last moment that I, as a German, was perhaps not trustworthy. I understood him; nevertheless, I had hoped that we might have been able to stay longer in Wrocław than a year, while I was working with the Poles.

Most of our things we left with Opa. I only took clothes for all of you, and Friedrich's letters from the years before the fortress period. At the station Opa pressed each of you to him and released you with a jerk. Last of all he took me in his arms and asked me to let him know if I managed to find Friedrich. As he walked away he kept stopping and turning round, until finally he turned down a street.

Only a day later our *trek* set off. We stayed overnight in a school near the station. It was mid-April and very mild, so we didn't need blankets. The following morning we climbed aboard one of the goods wagons. So as not to lose each other in the wagon, Rosa and I agreed on a certain signal – a whistle, which, as it turned out, was of little use amid the endless noise: the children's cries, the shouts, sobs and groans of the sick, the shrill whistle that the train driver blew before each departure, and the screeching of the train at every stop.

And then, ten days later, when we reached Hamburg, the opposite of what I expected happened: after we met your father again, suddenly I grew weaker and weaker. Your father did talk about seeing to an apartment for us together, but where was he going to get it? He said that a university in the East might possibly help him find one. I couldn't understand his confidence: the houses in the East were just as bomb-ravaged as those in the West. We would barely have survived the winter at the barracks: we would have had to steal coal, and there would surely have been arguments with the other families about how much coal each provided to heat the room. After only three weeks you fell ill, in sunny May. Luckily it was only a bad cough.

Perhaps I would have been less bothered by the camp had I not had this odd feeling. I could see that your father needed time to get used to our presence again; but I couldn't understand why he never invited us to his apartment during the day, or why he refused to put us up on the night of our arrival.

The woman he told me about some years later had at the time been very young and married to a man whom she more or less expected would return from the war. She had a five-year-old son. Your father said that he had meant to help her by looking after her child now and then, that she needed support. He told me he had intended to end it when my letter arrived, something he had hardly expected.

I asked him why he hadn't searched for us. His horror was genuine; you know, Margret, when you send a letter today, you don't question whether it will arrive...

In any case, lately there have indeed been problems with the post: two letters addressed to your father arrived from Switzerland with imperceptible tears and bends at the seals. Now that none of you live here any longer, I dedicate a lot of time to correspondence. I go out even less than before but write more letters than I did. Why would I write to you when you live in the same city? And Rosa has her husband. For me it is about the mental exchange. I would like your father to take me seriously. Not only do I write to friends but to newspapers as well. Then hundreds of people can read my lines. And I let authors know what I think of their books. If they write back, I leave the opened letter on the kitchen table so that your father sees it. How often do he and I speak? When he has visitors I frequently sit with them.

I scrutinise the letters addressed to him. Firstly, I cover up the addressee and try to decide whether the writing belongs to a woman or a man; then I feel the envelope's weight and contents before turning it over. Letters from men I take straight to his study.

So, when a second man's letter arrived with damaged seals, I knocked on his door. Your father ushered me in with a growl and almost tore the letter from my hands. He lowered his head over the page. I told him I would be concerned about these letters. He put down his pipe and waved his hand, as though he would shoo away a fly. The spring sun was shining in, and I saw the dust on the large windowpanes. To my right were his library shelves. From time to time I help to sort them when your father needs space for new books; otherwise, I set foot in his study as seldom as before.

"They want to be sure," he said to me, "we are in touch with the right people." He was serious.

"Doesn't it bother you that they read the thoughts that your colleagues abroad have addressed to you?"

"These are thoughts they would express publicly, at least in our country," he replied.

He seemed to be talking to himself rather than to me. He must have known I would question what he said. Twice a year we are visited by philosophers, physicists, chemists and sociologists from Munich, Locarno, Zurich and West Berlin. I smoke cigars with them, we get heady, drink the wine they bring, discuss and debate. None of these men would voluntarily leave their country to live with us here. While we tell them of job security and low rent, they shake their heads and say: your beloved Soviet Union waged war against you, too, like America against our people. Then Friedrich bangs his fist on the table, says you shouldn't compare the incomparable, and taps his wine glass for Marie to refill.

Before, when we had visitors, you girls scampered in and wanted to sit on my or your father's lap, but we sent you back to your rooms. During these evenings we spend with these well-travelled people, I forget my aches and pains because your father's presence bolsters me in the truest sense of the word. Even though he rarely returns my gaze, I feel a strange strength which lends my thoughts clarity and focus, and which allows me to express them in well-structured sentences; meanwhile, our different opinions seem to dissolve in the shared laughter I abandon myself to, as though this small smoky room filled with voices were the only place that existed. The room is scented with wine and I feel attractive and acknowledged. Do you know that, Margret? That for hours you can believe you are young? But you are still young. And soon will have a child yourself. Does it move? Yes?

Singing Soldiers

Hans • 1971

The ringing of the tram receded. Hans heard the steady stamping of drilling soldiers, briefly muffled by the screech of a tram turning a corner and the noise of two passing cars. To the left, his view of the soldiers was obscured by a high concrete wall, blackish green with moss and lichen near the ground and stained with mould higher up. Hans walked past the barrack gate, nodded to the Soviet guard and crossed the street over the tram tracks, briefly glancing up at the living room window as usual.

He climbed to the third floor and entered the apartment. Margret's hairbrush, her blue scarf, slips of paper, letters and some tram tickets were strewn on the hall bureau. The disorder irritated Hans. Margret regularly attended teaching conferences and party meetings, but it was rare that she came home later than him. Hans hung up his jacket and put down his briefcase on the hall stool then paced restlessly up and down in the living room.

He had found it hard to get used to their four-room city apartment. Three rooms led off the hall; Margret's small study directly adjoined the living room. Hans had argued at length with her over the need for it. He did not see why she needed a separate room for her lesson preparation. The day they moved in, she had ordered her writing desk be put in the small room, and Hans, to avoid argument in front of the removal man, had supervised with a mixture of impotence and anger.

He lingered a moment in the doorway to Margret's study then, like a scenting animal, prowled several times round the jotters, papers and books stacked on her desk.

On the other side of the apartment the evening sun was shining through the window of the virtually empty nursery. Hans looked out onto a drying green, a short steep grassy slope beyond and a new, pale yellow apartment block similar to theirs; to the left extended a play park bordered by snowberry bushes and fading buckthorn, with a rusty climbing frame, two swings, a wooden bridge to balance on and a sandpit. Hans turned away from the window. In a shaded corner stood a cot Margret had borrowed from a colleague; opposite, the long wall was obscured by two wardrobes of light veneer.

The soft-pile carpet deadened Hans's footsteps. The apartment was warm and dry, painted in white and filled with the smell of the new wardrobes. Even though they had lived here for over two years now, Hans still missed the slate shingles that covered his parents' house, as well as its kitsch interior: the gilt-edged vases, the lace doilies, the embroidered lace curtains, the flowery rugs and the photos in tarnished silver frames; he missed the worn sofa and the dark-brown furniture. At the same time, this plainly furnished apartment gave him a sense of relief.

He walked back into the living room, stood in front of the window and looked onto the tram tracks and the army barracks. Several bare-chested soldiers were marching smartly in line into one of the barrack buildings. Their torsos, pale, sallow or tanned, contrasted as markedly as their hair colour. Dust clouds billowed around their boots.

Hans heard the jangle of keys in the hall.

"Where were you?" he asked, turning swiftly to Margret.

"With my mother; she's got back pain again, and I gave her a little massage," Margret answered, and reached to hang up her jacket. She looked petite in spite of the visible bump under the loose, dark-blue shirt Hans had lent her this morning. The cuffs reached almost to her knuckles. He watched her as she efficiently tidied up, picked stray fluff from the carpet and finally stepped lightly through the hall. Her breasts had hardly grown during her pregnancy and she held herself straighter than before. The baby was due in the autumn, so there were around four months to go.

When she came up to him that first time on his evening winter walk, he had already thought then, how delicate and vulnerable she is! She had attracted him because he was frightened by the vigorous, unladylike way the young women from his village moved, lifted turnips from the earth, shouldered scythes and hoisted baskets of hay or apples. One day in the field he had watched one of them tie her headscarf, fast and furious and so tight, as though packaging up her own head. She wore a scarf of the kind his mother had an endless supply of and tied it the same way, even though she could barely have been twenty years old. Hans, aged fifteen, had felt both attracted and repelled by her. Later a wind had got up, and he had felt the cold at his hairline and ears, whereas the woman hardly seemed to notice.

Hans had also felt uncomfortable with Margret on that first evening. She knew how to choose her words and spoke without an accent. He had overcome his inhibition by talking, hardly letting her speak, and she had listened and responded without laughing at his dialect. Eventually Hans had relaxed and even offered her his gloves, although his heart raced as he did.

During the following weeks he had seen her several more times on the farm. He thought her pretty and a little aloof because she mostly kept apart from the others, as though she didn't wish to belong.

She rarely laughed – Hans never saw her raise her head to the farm labourers' banter – and, with lips pressed, quietly endeavoured to do her work well.

One afternoon he saw her carrying bags of manure from the delivery cart to the shed, while the others sniggered as they ate their packed lunch behind the building. After she had hoisted a sack onto her shoulder, Hans walked over and discreetly supported the underside. Even though Margret noticed and, with a nod, indicated he should go, Hans had remained, and later on he occasionally helped her with other jobs too. When she saw the ground she made up with his help, and that each time he left before the others came back, she quietly thanked him.

☙

Now, once more, Hans's feelings of tenderness towards Margret mingled with embarrassment. Sweating with excitement, he gingerly approached her as she opened the hall cupboard, pulled out the vacuum cleaner and leaned it against the living-room wall. He stepped up behind her, laid his hands on her warm belly and caressed it.

For a moment Margret stopped, seemed to freeze; then, slowly but surely, she reached for the vacuum cleaner, and Hans withdrew his hands. Her expression stern, almost obstinate, she quickly passed the grey machine over her study carpet.

Not for the first time, Hans felt a desire to hurt her. One evening two years ago, Margret had persuaded him to go dancing. Around midnight the dancers jostled with flushed faces at the cloakroom and, when it was Hans's turn, he had collected their coats and handed her hers outside. "A man should help a woman on with her coat," she lectured him, explaining that it was part of a cultured upbringing. Hans had smiled, but Margret gave him a withering look. He could find nothing to say in defence.

Hans often asked himself if it was his fault that she rebuffed him, that now she laughed as little as when they had first met, as rarely as his mother. But Hans, unlike his father, did not need looking after, and he loved Margret, but differently – it seemed to him – to how she wished him to love her. She was hardly interested in his affections yet showed him evidence of her pupils' affection – pictures and birthday cards – with the same pride with which she told him about the influence she had on them, and how much she cared about children who were neglected by their parents. Sometimes Hans thought she acted like an abandoned child herself, reliant upon the approval and goodwill of other people who never came too close.

However, it affected him less than before.

଼ଠ

Wrenched from his thoughts by Margret's voice, Hans realised he was staring at his empty hands. Hurriedly he stuck them in his pockets.

Margret was talking about her father. Her mother had just told her that Friedrich would soon receive the *Nationalpreis*†. Her voice swelled with pride and importance.

As Hans searched for words to convey his appreciation, he pictured her parents' house and recalled the first time Margret had suggested they visit Friedrich and Johanna. Upon entering and looking around, Hans had been struck by its spaciousness. The household help carried coffee and warm, sweet-smelling cherry cake on a tray into the living room adjoining the library. Hans and Margret followed her into the parlour-like room. Margret's parents were seated at either end of a long table that would easily have sat ten. They had taken their seats like royalty, one of whom had been invited here from a faraway kingdom. Her mother stood up and announced in an unnaturally high voice, "So, our girl comes to visit!"

When Margret introduced Hans, her mother looked at him and said, "Ah, yes, the boyfriend. How do you do?"

She nodded to him. Margret's father, however, stood up, smoothed his suit, walked over to Hans and held out his hand. "Welcome to our house."

Hans shook his soft, slender hand, which was like a woman's. Hans's father had broad, hairy hands.

After the meal, Margret's father led Hans into the room that housed the library. Reverently, as though entering a church, Hans stepped into the darkened room suffused with the smell of tobacco smoke. Lined up before him were endless rows of dark shelves. Never before had he seen so many books in one house.

Hans thought of the cramped living-room-cum-kitchen where his mother baked, cooked, cleaned and dusted, and which no one – neither his father, his mother, nor Hans himself – usually left before ten at night. In that kitchen they had talked about illnesses, children, the war, the harvest, food, the weather. Even though his father and mother had been good pupils, no one had discussed books at home.

As Margret's father was stacking several volumes on botany on his desk, from the garden Margret knocked on the windowpane. Over coffee she had hardly spoken, yet now she seemed cheerful and childlike. When Hans opened the door to the garden, Margret took him by the hand, gently pulled him a little way from the door and kissed him. Although they stood kissing up against the wall, Hans feared her parents would see them. But Margret led him farther, to a hazelnut bush, and she gathered the nuts in her skirt pocket, bending tirelessly and whispering to him to help.

In her parents' garden, so it seemed to Hans to this day, Margret smiled with the air of someone immersed in happy memories.

∞

Since that afternoon Hans had spoken frequently with Friedrich. Their conversations made him think more carefully about why he wanted to be a biologist. Hans already enjoyed conducting research, fascinated by the myriad structures revealed under the microscope. Usually his hand was unsteady when dissecting the body parts of dead animals, even just a fly wing, but to plants he applied the razor blade unhesitatingly.

In the forest around the university town the trees did not grow thickly together, instead enclosed meadows here and there. Sometimes Hans went on solo field trips, in one day walking round half the city, or else he took one of the local trains that ran on a single track and stopped everywhere. Then he would get out at a station with a tiny signal box and walk along golden, dark-green or earth-brown fields to woods or meadows that had been recommended to the students.

When gathering plants for his herbarium, Hans would carefully dig them out by the roots, label each with its location and date, place them in one plastic bag, and only later when he stopped to rest would he put them in his plant press consisting of two sheets of strong card and newspaper. If he found an unusual plant, he at once looked up his Rothmaler field guide for its name; otherwise, he waited until he was home to identify it.

For his floristic survey he used a topographical map, painstakingly recording every location and plant prevalence, as only in this way could he discover which plants grew in the area and bore a close association.

Back from his outings, Hans enjoyed the peace and concentration with which he could at last set about his task. Of far more interest to him than the field work was this systematic work, the taxonomy of the plants, and he loved to compare their characteristics, learning from an early stage that isolated incidences of similarity did not necessarily predicate a relationship; however, where two plants showed several basic similarities, you could often assume a common origin.

Eagerly Hans studied the specimens he brought back from his walks and one morning realised that identifying similarities caused him happy palpitations, whereas variations, which were just as conducive to his research work, he recorded with indifference. That day Hans had doubted his talent for science, but not even the temporary fatigue he had felt for the first time soon after that could bring him to abandon his studies. Although it was customary (and often boring for him) to continually recheck long-exhausted research, Hans knew he wished to study no other subject.

Whilst he deepened his knowledge by the day, he began to dream that after his studies he would find the right places for newly discovered plants in the system of kingdoms, classes, subclasses, orders, families, genus and species, and bring to light as yet unidentified interrelationships.

An interest, Friedrich had told him, could not be sufficient motive; young people today were being granted an opportunity denied their parents: practically an entire lifetime without war, a new beginning in a country that needed its people – a country for which it was worth living.

Hans found his own, unfinished thoughts echoed in Friedrich's words. Secretly he suspected his father's illness was a consequence of the war, even though no doctor could confirm his suspicion. His mother had borne him during the war; for three years he had lived alone with her.

Later, when his father told him about Finland where, far from the reality of war, he had been drilled and trained in machine guns, cannons, hand grenades and armoured vehicles, Hans's stomach would tighten in fear. Other men in the village, his father would continue dismissively, had been robbed of their tongue; other men had lost a leg, or both legs; other men sat in the pub night after night.

It gave Hans goose bumps to walk through the village past these silent men, who either had a wooden leg or not. Often he heard their drunken hollering echo through the village.

Once or twice as a student, Hans had had the vague hope he could one day help his father by inventing a new drug; but then, as his studies drew to an end, he wondered how best he could serve his country with his work. Here it was about more than the life of one person.

80

Soundlessly Margret entered the living room, a shadow Hans might not have noticed had her voice, clear and matter-of-fact, not reached him. "The spin-dryer won't work."

She stood before him with wet, reddened hands, the sleeves of his shirt rolled above her elbows. Hans nodded and looked at her expectantly.

"Can you please try to fix it?" Margret said impatiently.

In the bathroom Hans bent over the knee-high, cylindrical machine and slid the grey lever fully across to the centre of the lid. The machine failed to vibrate as he had expected, so Hans returned the lever. When the spin-dryer was on, it made your arms shake when you pressed down on the lever and held the drum at the same time. The design was basic; water ran into the sink via a rubber hose.

Hans pulled out the plug and opened the drum, which contained a dark, drenched heap of washing. He sensed Margret beside him lift out the heavy garments and deposit them in the bath. Over the dark pile he saw her blonde hair. There was a tension between their bodies like before a boxing match. The water seeping from the washing formed small pools on the tiles. Although neither of them spoke, it seemed to Hans as though even in their silence Margret was disturbed by his presence.

He examined the drum's grey rubber inner seal (this looked intact) and its flat metal bottom; he inspected the cable and checked the machine was sitting level, before plugging it in again and turning the lever to the middle.

At a loss, apologetically he looked to Margret. She stood with her hands on her slender hips and glared back angrily. "Leave it, you can't do it; I'll go over to Wagner's," she said.

As he stood up, Hans felt dizzy. A vague, blurry image came to mind: a meadow, and a goat he was meant to milk; nearby his mother, scolding him when the goat ran away.

Ten minutes later Margret returned with the neighbour.

"You know," she said, as she pressed herself up against the wide-open door and invited him in with a courteous wave, "my husband's from the village, they don't have spin-dryers there yet."

The neighbour laughed, and Hans, who had been about to nod to him from the hall, turned away with a red face and clenched his fists. Out of the corner of his eye he saw as Margret took the neighbour familiarly by the arm and led him into the bathroom. Through the open nursery door Hans's gaze fell on the cot. He walked along the hall into the living room and stood at the window.

Below, the soldiers were sitting in a circle on the bare ground singing a Russian folk song in deep voices. Hans gulped as tears came into his eyes.

Silent Christmas

Margret • 1971

The people seemed to have retreated to their flats, to their families; even the army barracks looked deserted. Margret went through to the kitchen and gazed out the window to the forest, where the paths must have been dry and firm as neither rain nor snow had fallen in recent weeks.

While Hans walked up there on the hill and Sonja slept in her cot in the nursery, a singular silence reigned in the apartment. Margaret stirred a big pot simmering with sauerkraut. She had not asked her mother, or Marie (who prepared Christmas dinner every year), for the recipe. She wiped her brow because steam was getting in her face. Should she add the juniper berries now or later? Undecided, she turned to the other pot, which had froth bubbling over its side, lifted the lid, turned down the gas and gripped the pot by the handles. She let out a quiet cry, bit her lips and ran her fingers under cold water. Although redness remained, gradually the pain diminished.

Margret dried off her hands on the tea towel, took the oven cloth and poured the potatoes. Why had her anxiety not gone, today of all days, when she and Hans were set to celebrate their first Christmas without their parents? They were a family now, as they had wished; all the same, Margret felt no particular sense of joy. As she visualised Hans wandering among the trees (even in winter he examined their branches, sometimes broke some off and explored them at various points with his fingers), nearing the summit along narrow serpentine forest tracks, paths Margret knew and liked to walk, she wondered why she felt no desire to accompany him.

∞

She heard Sonja crying quietly and glanced at the kitchen clock: it was after five and the little thing needed her dinner. Strange how quickly she got used to her mealtimes.

The pan for the white sausage was already on the hob, leaving one ring to warm Sonja's bottle. When Margret put a match to the ring, the flame flared blue and orange before settling evenly around the grey burner. She set a water-filled pot on top, inserted the bottle and intermittently tested the temperature. Eventually she lifted Sonja from her cot. She felt almost weightless, a little shut-eyed worm that gurgled greedily as she guzzled the porridge-like liquid in the bottle. It felt strange, lovely and new to think that her baby would be at home for two whole weeks. Margret watched Sonja drink and stroked her head from time to time.

A month ago she had taken Sonja to *crèche*[†] for the first time. Her daughter was eight weeks old and Margret was missing school; she was looking forward to her lessons, her work, her professional duties. The *crèche* leader all but snatched Sonja out of her arms, the way you purposefully take someone's bag to be helpful. Margret was aware of a wrenching pain similar to the one she had felt in the hours immediately after Sonja's birth, when she had lain exhausted but wide awake alongside other mothers in a room on the maternity ward without her daughter who, her entire body yellow, had been taken to the children's clinic.

Margret cast a cursory glance round the *crèche*, saw little white jackets, rompers and nappies, white walls, a hard changing table, shelves, drawers, some colourful plastic rattles, infant faces red from bawling, as tiny and tender as Sonja's, the severe faces of women. She could smell the laundry room with its doors ajar, a pail full of nappies, prepared milk formula. Margret felt sick and quickly said goodbye.

Her anxiousness only eased in class as a pupil recited a poem. The girl was wearing her white Pioneer[†] blouse with a red kerchief because Monday was roll call day. Margret could see the pupil was striving for the right emphasis without being fully engaged, but even so she felt the poem speak about her and Sonja, about how they were people amongst other people and thus part of a community. Margret felt the power emanate from the lines – "Onwards! Do your duty!" – as, with her eyes fastened on the badge of her pupil's Pioneer blouse, she disregarded the girl's expression.

When Margret fetched Sonja that afternoon, in the main room entrance she chatted with another mother, guardedly at first; then, while the *crèche* leader put fresh nappies on the woman's child, she gained confidence as she heard how natural it had become for this other woman to leave her baby there.

With every day, Margret grew more used to depositing Sonja at *crèche*. When she collected her late in the afternoon she always discussed with the leader how much her daughter had drunk, how much her weight had increased by, and together they studied the carefully completed chart on the grey board above Sonja's little bed – the same charts that were mounted above the other babies' beds. Sonja developed and thrived, one of many babies; she grew stronger, her cheeks rosier, and sometimes she cried when the nurse handed her back to Margret.

∞

Margret spread a cloth nappy over her shoulder, lifted Sonja whilst supporting her head with one hand and patted her back several times. A little light fluid ran soundlessly onto the cloth. During her feed Sonja briefly woke then instantly fell asleep again. Margret carried her back into the nursery and laid her in her cot.

As she turned round she gave a start. She had failed to hear Hans come in. He was standing in the door with ruddied cheeks, smiling, relaxed.

"She's asleep," Margret said, and walked towards him to leave the room. She thought of Sonja's yet-to-be-sorted rompers piled in the laundry basket, her yet-to-be-washed nappies, and the meal. His head resting on the crook of his arm, Hans leaned against one side of the door frame, filling it almost entirely. When Margret was directly in front of him, he lifted his other arm to clasp her round the waist.

"Can you please let me past?" Margret asked, whereupon Hans let his arm fall and pressed himself up against the door frame. She saw in his face the hurt she had caused, and she thought that she ought to be happy; and she also thought of her strange desire to flee whenever Hans stood before her, looked at her or made to touch her. He seemed another person to the one she had once got to know; now, his gentleness often felt like weakness, and the fact that he was well read despite his background had yet to have any significant bearing on their daily lives. Margret could not understand why so little remained of her earlier infatuation, and it saddened her.

In the kitchen she shook some almost black juniper berries into her palm and picked up one that was still soft, not yet fully dried, between her thumb and forefinger, and pressed firmly until the berry burst and the skin slipped from its golden-brown interior. She added the rest to the sauerkraut.

In the living room stood a small straight spruce that three days ago Hans had bought and fixed in a tree stand. Margret could easily touch the top. As of next year, Hans had said, each Christmas they would buy a tree slightly taller than last year's, to match the children's growth. Stowed in cardboard boxes beside the tree were the decorations they had borrowed for a few days. Margret opened them: red and purple glittering baubles from Lene; from Margret's colleague, metal candle holders showing signs of rust; from Hans's colleagues, a small carton filled with hand-crafted figures made of modelling clay and raffia.

Hans came into the room. Margret heard him approach, glanced up, saw that he had changed and was smoothing his suit in expectation. She could not help but smile, for he came across as a big boy. But he did not arouse her affection. She nodded in reply to his tacit question as to whether he looked good in his suit. Then she dipped her hand into an assortment of figures that looked to have been made by children, found a little man who resembled a marionette (albeit his arms and legs did not move) and a finger-sized Pinocchio with a delicate nose, which she hung on an upper branch. The needles pricked as she slipped the thread over. Hans bent down and began to hang the baubles; with care he distributed them evenly over the tree whilst Margret attended to the stars, moons and small animals, the clown and the snowman; lastly, together they attached the candle holders and set white candles in them. Reverently Margret held a burning match to the first wick. Her gaze was transfixed by the unexpectedly tall flame with soot rising from the tip. The flame flickered softly and cast a strong shifting shadow on the wall.

One by one Margret lit the other candles. For a moment the smell of spent matchsticks seemed to overpower the aroma of food. As Margret untied her apron and gazed at the candle lights, then at the red bauble at the top of the tree, she remembered she had a dress of the same bright colour, and that she still had to change.

When she came back into the living room, in a dark-blue dress, Hans handed her a parcel. It was the same shape as a large book, but felt softer. Margret thanked him and laid it on the dinner table while she went to get Hans's present from her study. She handed it to him with outstretched arm.

"And where will we put Sonja's present?" Hans asked.

"In her cot," Margret replied.

Together they had bought Sonja a sky-blue teddy bear with a fluffy coat, about the same size as her; it had been the last one in the shop, the one that had persuaded passers-by to come in: the bear in the window. Sonja would grow up with it and outgrow it, but the bear too would change; its coat would grow tattered and stained from the marks left by Sonja, while all the time she grew ever fonder of it.

Sonja lay on her back in the cot with eyes closed, tiny yellow crusty specks stuck to her all-but-invisible eyelashes. Almost inaudibly she snored. The white feather duvet, tucked in at the sides, left her head, shoulders and arms free. Margret would have liked to lift her out and cuddle her, but did not want to waken her. Hans leaned over the cot and carefully placed the teddy bear on the puffy duvet. Sonja remained motionless and Hans straightened again. He looked pensive, unhappy; finally, he slid the soft toy onto Sonja's arm next to her head. Sonja opened her hand slightly and involuntarily waved her fingers in the air without reaching for the teddy.

For a time Hans and Margret stood silently by the cot before returning to the living room. Still in silence they loosened the ribbons round their presents and unwrapped them. Uncertainly Hans held the smart light-grey corduroy shirt with pearl buttons that Margret had bought him up against his chest, and smiled at her. Then, with surprisingly swift motion, he took off his jacket and shirt and slipped the new one over his pale, dark-haired skin. Margret gulped; flustered by the sudden sight of his nakedness, she briskly busied herself with her own present, folding back the sheet of wrapping paper to reveal three thick numbered booklets.

"I thought the book might interest you," Hans said, "though I haven't read it myself. The shop had sold out, so I borrowed it and transcribed it."

On the top booklet, the large capital letters that spelled the title – *The Deputy** – looked stencilled. Margret had once heard her parents talk about the play. Speechless, she leafed through the booklet; both sides of each sheet were covered in Hans's minute, meticulous handwriting in dark-blue pen. She read a few lines and wondered how many evenings Hans had spent writing without her knowing. He was standing next to the tree, fastening his belt over the new shirt. She went over to him, saw him look up in surprise and pressed him close to her. He seemed big and gentle; his cheeks were smooth and cool, the skin on his neck rough. She felt him return her embrace as he clasped her above her hips, without caressing her. The pressure of his warm hands felt nice and slightly disconcerting.

Hans was first to remove his hands and take a step back.

"I think Sonja's woken up," he said softly.

Margret nodded, still half leaning against his shoulder. She was both sorry and glad he had not tried to kiss her.

They moved apart, he to the nursery, she to the kitchen, where Margret tied her apron over her dress. She placed the sausages in the pan then began to mash the potatoes, added milk and nutmeg, turned the sausages then carried on mashing. After a while her arms grew tired and she called Hans. When he didn't reply she went along the hall and stopped at the living room door. Hans was standing in front of the Christmas tree with Sonja on his arm. With his thumb and forefinger he was holding a yellowish figure and gently telling Sonja the story of the snowman who was afraid of spring until he heard that, after transforming three times, he would return to his field the following winter. Sonja gazed at the figure and moved her lips; a thin thread of saliva ran down her chin. Hans's voice rang soothingly as he spoke now to Sonja, now to the figure, and, after he had finished the last sentence – *And the snowman was comforted and calmly awaited his transformations** – he showed Sonja little Pinocchio with his shiny protruding nose, a slender red stick. Carefully Hans guided Sonja's finger to the figure; she reached for it, and her hand gave such a jerk that the nose broke off. Instinctively Hans put his hand round hers; briefly he swore, prized open her fist and took the figure from her. He noticed Margret at the door, held out Sonja to her and sullenly lowered his head over the broken Pinocchio.

"Let me fix it," Margret said, taking the baby on her arm and the figure in her hand.

As she turned off the last ring in the kitchen, she remembered the almost spent candles. She went into the living room and blew them out, one by one. As smoke arose, Margret lit a fresh candle from the last one still burning and set it into soft wax.

The Greatest of Joys

Erwin • 1972

One day the wee one will cross the globe, she's so bright and curious. Around she wriggles on my lap, grabs my nose, gurgles with delight and reaches out her arms to the grass. Soon she will set my buggy going. I tickle her ear one last time, hold her aloft, press her soft cheek to mine and say to her quietly but clearly, "Oh-pah," before I pass her to Margret, who sets her down on the lawn. The wee thing crawls towards the garden gate.

Even in the shade it's hot. Lene wipes her forehead with her handkerchief and goes into the house. Hans gazes over absently to the woods as Margret crouches in front of the garden gate, arms outstretched for Sonja, who crawls squealing towards her.

A funny wee scamp like that is the greatest joy on earth. And that I'm still able to see, feel and hold Sonja is *my* greatest joy. Though it was only one time that joy truly deserted me.

I never had to shoot anyone in the Finnish forests and came back unscathed to the district: to where I grew up, and where we still live today. Our uniforms we happily and hastily tore off and exchanged for civilian things with a farmer's wife whose husband had been killed. And then we walked and walked, three men from neighbouring villages, until we met the Americans. On that occasion too I had some joy, because they only took me prisoner for a few days.

Then, when I stepped from the dense forest into our village fields, squinted, sighed, breathed in the country air and finally opened my eyes, some twenty metres away bent over the grass was a young woman. She squatted, grasped a clump of grass and tore it out. The boy beside her was picking yellow plants – I thought of arnica-soaked dressings on war wounds – when he looked over. A faint word reached me on the next breeze. Hans recognised me first, although he was barely three years old.

Lene straightened beside him. I ran towards them waving my arms, and when I made to press them to me, I almost knocked them over. After we had embraced, I sensed Lene study me with a smile. As I shouldered the basket half-filled with grass and said I wanted to go home, Hans offered me his wee yellow flowers.

Our home looked just as clean and tidy as on my last visit. There was a place for everything: my trousers and Lene's dresses hung in the bedroom wardrobe, the crockery stood on the kitchen sideboard; there was a scent of soap. We men hadn't boasted such cleanliness. Hans was wearing bright knitted socks with ribs that tightly hugged his calves. I knew Lene had waited for me.

ꚙ

As a young girl Lene was always brave and helpful, and for a long time happy, until her mother suddenly fainted and never woke again. After her mother's death I saw Lene distraught, crying for days. All the same, day after day at dawn she would walk the forest path over to the glassworks in the next village. Sometimes I broke off from my work to watch her hurry past our glass-blowing studio; always she walked briskly and looked straight ahead. When I visited her in the evening for half an hour, mostly she would be sitting in the front room, her head bent over some sewing or knitting. Her three younger sisters would fall silent as soon as I entered. Their father often only returned home at night. I only asked Lene one or two times if she wanted to go to the cinema. After that I got into the habit of visiting her at home. Each time, she would stop her work and give me a plate of bread and sausage. When she cleared away my plate, I knew I had to go.

For me, Lene was the prettiest girl in the village. I liked her face and her laugh, but her strength of movement attracted me much more. She could have walked as far as the sea, shovelled coal for ten families or even mined iron ore… Her laughter is gone, but her energy endures: how she stoops and tugs on a potato plant; how she stirs the soup in the pan more rigorously than before and quite differently to Hans, who goes over a potato three times before gingerly removing the earth. He has become a scholar, as we had wished: because back then, I'd already noticed how he liked to collect and arrange plants. Of course, Hans was always hungry as a young boy and gobbled down everything edible – potatoes, bread and firm sharp fruit – but later he would compare the colour and size of apples, weigh their seeds, press sorrel or dandelion leaves (which formerly he would have chewed, then gulped down) and small flowers that grew in the grass. Before he mounted his dried plants, with his newly sharpened pencil he would draw a frame for each on the paper; measure out the corners with a triangle and protractor, rub out any superfluous lines and grow angry if a plant didn't fit in its frame.

When Hans was in first or second grade, sometimes after work I would pick up him and Lene from my father-in-law's farm, and one time I watched as he dreamily scraped the earth from a potato, moving his lips as he did, almost as though he were chewing with his mouth closed. He swallowed, stopped, looked to Lene and finally put the potato in the basket. In her pinafore, Lene carried her picked potatoes to this same basket, froze, studied the top layer, fished out the clean potatoes and said impatiently, "Potatoes must not be cleaned!"

Hans turned red and hurriedly bent down for more.

I liked it when we walked home together in the evening and Hans ran round me, raced ahead and shouted for me to catch him. Despite our exhaustion we were happy, and when I took Lene by the waist and with a skip turned her in polka step, she would laugh and give me a kiss on the nose or the mouth; until one day as we danced I felt a tingle in my calves, to which at first I paid no heed. Only minutes later my muscles went into a spasm, as though trying to lead their own dance. The closer summer drew, the less they obeyed me. In the end, before Lene spoke with the village doctor, I crawled the last bit of the way on the dry earth, not unlike the way Sonja shuffles forwards today.

೮

Now the wee one is crawling off in the other direction. Were she to climb over the fence, after five hundred metres she would come to the gates to the mine, which will soon be shut. Lene mopped up the miners' dirt from the plant floor, but Sonja will follow in her parents' footsteps; the village will get smaller and smaller and eventually disappear altogether; even if our neighbours' children stay here, their children will leave. I don't know if I am sad about it. If our grandchildren are all right, we have to be content at the end of the time granted to us.

I was never down the mine. Each morning the men from the work settlement bid farewell to their families. Always heartfelt – after all, you never know what'll happen to you at depth. From the window we see them embrace, hear their children's cries. Some have lived in the settlement for ten years, others more than twenty, like us. When Lene fell pregnant a second time, the house was leased to us. Although she lost the child before it was born, we continued to live there and didn't have to negotiate with anyone when more miners moved into the area;

no one in the village would have approved if a stranger had driven a paraplegic out of his house.

But now the ore is almost exhausted. The screeching of the trolleys behind our house has always accompanied us as we get up in the morning and go to work, when we come home and when we go to bed. I hardly used to bat an eyelid. Now I keep an ear out for it again and notice how the intervals between trolleys are lengthening. Some days the men come home earlier; sometimes I meet one or two in the early afternoon on the street or outside the *Konsum*. Their hands and faces are clean, newly washed, their hair combed, clothes fresh and ironed; all the same, some behave like they have just woken up: they squint, stagger, suddenly stop. They remind me of moles trying to find their bearings above ground. Others are lively and talkative, greet me with a slap on the shoulder, walk for a bit beside my buggy and tell me they are going to change jobs, give up their house, move away. Outside the *Konsum* people wait and whisper about who is to stay and who is to go. Contented smiles play on their lips; they nod in agreement. The miners cannot understand what is said: pneumatic hammers have given them deaf ears.

I have got into the habit of being out. Greet everyone with a wave, thank those who help me if my buggy suddenly stops or I have to use the toilet. Why would I envy the neighbours anything? We have a roof over our heads, more to eat than ever before, the most beautiful grandchild in the world. Of course, I don't know how I can ever thank Lene. There are times when I want to kiss her like before, when I was a young man, to bring back her laughter, but she is very focused on what she does and won't rest until all her jobs are done. Doesn't bother me that I am part of her round of tasks. She hasn't forgotten that my heart and mind are just as alive as before.

ॐ

Once, five years ago – the doctors had all but given up on me – my brother came to visit. He lives two villages on in a slate house in the valley. I was barely a week out of hospital when he rang at our door, stumbled over his hello (because I was laughing) and hurriedly stuffed some papers back in his jacket pocket. Then he told us how a few comrades from the district authorities had decided to install wide ramps for wheelchairs at all the major shops. Lene fed and watered him, as she did all our guests, and he wolfed down his food without so much as a thank you, then bade us goodbye. At the door Lene whispered something to him. I only caught fragments of what she said. That night in bed I sat up, turned, reached out my arms and pressed my palms to the floor. When my legs hit the floor Lene woke up. She berated me; I cursed. I told her I no longer wanted to be a millstone.

"You are my husband," she answered me.

Although I'm not sure if Margret would say the same to Hans, she seems a good wife for him; a little too delicate, but smart and sensible; a dutiful teacher and a contented mother.

When Hans was still wee I came home once a year on leave. I cannot remember if he crawled through the grass, got the bottle or the breast, gurgled or quietly chuckled or didn't laugh at all. He always wore things Lene had knitted: little jackets, breeks with knitted braces, stockings and hats. A wee bundle of white and blue wool that we tucked up in bed with a blanket. Just his nose peeped out. I remember there was often a smell under the blanket after his sleep, because I had to rinse his nappies. Girls are cleaner, Lene says.

Margret waves this aside when I tell her. "A baby's a baby," she replies.

She turns to Hans, who launches Sonja into the air once or twice and catches her. He comes over and places the wee thing in my arms. This time she nestles into my elbow and yawns with her all-but-toothless mouth. I won't have to go through my teeth falling out again or eating mashed-up food. Gently I remove Sonja's hat and stroke her downy hair until her eyelids fall shut. Hans smiles at me.

No, it's not the same whether you raise a girl or a boy. I would have liked to play football with Hans more, teach him how you kick the ball into the top corner, how you chop wood, stack it smartly and carry it correctly; would have liked to race him when he was young beyond the forest to the next village and back. I'd have lured him away from his herbaria and his books, spiced up his strolls.

I should have also told him what it's like when you become a man, but could hardly recall it, a dim and distant feeling, unreal like the short spell afterwards when I slept with women. Yes, I knew a few before Lene, but what does that mean now? While Hans grew to be a young man I was already living like an oldie, immobile from the waist down. I felt ashamed, and ashamed in front of Hans, and said nothing.

Sometimes, before he went to sleep, Hans would ask if he couldn't work with me in the glassworks instead of on the farm or in the field.

"Later," I replied. "Maybe later."

Often when I fetched him and Lene, he presented me with a flower, a beetle, a worm or an ant. Sundays in church he would forever plead to be allowed to sit beside me; later, every Sunday morning he would hold now one, now the other armrest of my buggy, incessantly ask questions (which I couldn't always think of an answer to right away), tell riddles so I didn't get bored, or else bring me something to drink. Lene hurried us along, said she wanted to be in time for intercession, that the boy still had to get changed and comb his hair. I avoided confrontation with Lene. Even on Sundays she would get up at six o'clock, wash the floor on her knees, make the coffee, feed the animals, fetch me a wash basin and cloth, and pull up my trousers so I could button them.

I ask myself if Lene needs my help in the house. Often I peel the potatoes or roll out the pasta dough for lunch. In my seat I press the rolling pin to the solid lump. The potatoes we have been buying from the *Konsum* for a few years now are less work than those from the garden and my father-in-law's field, because they are bigger and cleaner. But they taste drier. The last remaining potato plants in our garden only suffice for a few meals each year.

I wave to Hans. Unmistakably I feel Sonja's weight, lying on my lap with her legs tucked, fingers bunched, nose buried in my shirt. Hans puts on her hat, pushes her pram into the shade and lays her down in it. Even though no sun strikes her face, he protectively raises the hood of the pram.

∞

With barely a sound I drive to the house along our slab path. Hans stoops over the slabs at some spots and studies them with a faintly knitted brow, as though he must stop himself from kneeling down and shifting one or two a fraction. At the time I wanted to do the work alone, but now it strikes me that Hans and I have made something that serves us all, even Sonja, whose pram rolls over the stone path as effortlessly as my buggy.

Hans opens the door and calls to Lene, who brings us a chair. Before he lifts me out of my buggy I turn to Sonja, who, newly awoken, babbles to herself and beams at Margret. As Margret points towards me, Sonja gurgles and spreads her fingers in the air as if waving.

She shall one day go and explore the Finnish forests – where they shoot no more – the lakes and mountains and towns that we never saw... but before that, sure as sure, it'll be I who go.

It's not about Fun

Lene • 1975

I wouldn't have been able to pay for a special stone. Nor did I wish to draw attention, stand out from the neighbours; which is why I chose the same grey granite with the gold lettering as for my father and had the name engraved at the same height, only leaving out the cross above because Erwin wished it thus.

It's important the flowers are always fresh. A few years ago I stuck a calendar page on white card, with the message that flowers on graves are no use to anyone, and mounted it in a gilt frame. But is it not a person's duty to maintain their relatives' resting places?

In the garden I cut bright red chrysanthemums for Erwin's grave, white for my father's. How often I have walked up the path through the meadows to the paternal farm that lies beyond the graveyard at the forest edge – and should have been mine, because I am the eldest. But with a sick man you learn to do without.

With a plastic vase in each hand I hurry along the pebble path to the little graveyard fountain, fill each vase with rainwater and stick the prong of the first one in the ground in front of my father's gravestone. Then I take the other vase to Erwin's grave. The big chrysanthemum heads shine and seem too heavy to sway in the wind: a thought that wouldn't have entered my head before. I breathe slower and sit for a moment on the small green seat by the fence, so that the time passes and I remember that none of us needs to hurry.

On the day my mother died I rushed from house to house to tell the news, and where they let me in, they held their hands to their faces. As soon as they tried to take me in their arms I said I had to keep going. At home my sisters cried, I comforted them, encouraged them to eat something, sang the two wee ones a lullaby, gave the older one a kiss and put an arm around her. Only once all three were asleep did I go to bed and quietly cry.

I don't recall that I cried again later. Wouldn't have been time for that, anyway. Now here I sit on this seat slightly away from the gravestones, a few metres from the high forest, and think of my flowerbeds that have to be covered in winter, the redcurrants to be sugared and boiled, the red and white wool for the hat I want to knit for Sonja, the wood to be stacked, the sausage I'll buy and keep in the cellar because it's the one Hans likes best, the fruit crumble cake for my neighbour in case she should knock at my door.

As I stand up I briefly turn round. The forest seems to wave with swaying needle branches, like hands that come closer and draw me back to the seat. Yes, it's true; I have time to listen to the sounds of the forest.

∞

In those days I wore long plaits that my mother, my grandmother or one of the girls from school wove for me, plaits that bounced as I walked and brushed the ground as I foraged for mushrooms and berries in the forest. Broad were the paths we strolled along, boys and girls arm in arm, side by side; and in summer, sunlight spilled through the leaves and dappled the ground. Dry or damp, the forest was fragrant with mushrooms, trees, moss, wild herbs, shallow stream water. I remember the old folk song: *When everything comes to life again / the earth flourishes fresh and green / the lark arises in the sky / with joyous bright melodic cry**. Previously my voice rang clear, but never as loud as the other children's. I search for the words to the second verse, but they don't come to mind.

A share of the berries we sold to the village's old folk, whose children and grandchildren hadn't time for gathering because they had to work. On market days my mother carried the remaining berries in tin pails to the bus that went into town twice a day. Every week she would give me fifty pfennigs from the proceeds. Every Sunday I would buy a ticket for the cinema, sit in the front row next to Hella and Werner from my class and hum along to the songs the projectionist played on the gramophone.

Erwin always sat in one of the back rows, and we girls turned and giggled at this young man who went to the cinema alone. Later, after I had left school, sometimes my route past the village glass-blowing studio coincided with the end of his working day. Erwin spoke disparagingly of the machines we worked at in the glassworks. Would we not turn into machines ourselves, he asked, in that chilly atmosphere, forever loading and unloading the tubes?

I hadn't even thought about it because I was happy to be earning money for my family. Erwin invited me to watch him at his work, and when a few days later I passed the glass-blowing studio again, after a moment's hesitation I knocked on the door.

Little flames flickered at various spots in the room. Erwin turned his head, scarcely seemed surprised, looked really focused.

"Sit you down, girl, on yon chair," he said.

Beads of sweat ran past his eyes down his cheeks. I sat so I could watch his hands and face in profile. In the flame glowed a blue ball of glass that Erwin turned on a pole. The moment the glass became soft and limp and threatened to fall off, Erwin put the pole to his mouth. Like a trumpet player, his cheeks filled with air as the gleaming ball expanded and changed in shape. Erwin's hands were big and strong, the myriad veins standing out markedly; lovely hands that nevertheless belied their agility. Erwin's face looked serious, engrossed; I gazed at him so long I missed the final stage of his work. He hid a smile as he stood up and carefully carried the almost finished phial before him to the oven. Like his hands, his body was strong; his grey work overalls and coarsely woven shirt made him look younger than he did in the Sunday suit he usually wore to the cinema. I too had on my plain weekday dress; folded inside my pocket was my faded, checked work overall, which my mother used to wear over her dress as she rubbed washing on the washboard.

"Wait a moment, girl," Erwin said.

He disappeared into a small side room; when, after a while, he came back, he smelled faintly of soap. Outside, he reached for my hand, and, although I gulped in surprise, I only took my fingers from his when we neared my house.

ဆ

Then other children crowded into the front row of the cinema. My school friends sat as awkwardly beside their young beaus as I beside Erwin, or else they stayed away from the cinema, like the boys. Sat next to Erwin I would never have sung along to one of the songs, even though he himself hummed softly to the music.

One day our projectionist removed the gramophone, but still music echoed in the dim auditorium. Erwin and I stared at the actors' mouths, and I knew not whether to listen or to look. Occasionally I missed some of the story because I was entranced by the sound of their voices.

In one of the films – I remember it well – a young woman married a good-looking gentleman who owned a farm the size of a village. The woman wore an ankle-length, figure-hugging dress. During their first kiss the sun shone so brightly, yet the woman's dark hair remained in rings on her smooth forehead with not a bead of sweat visible. And although for the wedding the servants slaughtered pigs and hens, cooked the meat in the kitchen, made dough and stirred sauces, they walked around the whole time in spotless clothing.

The morning of my wedding I baked a redcurrant cake with the eldest of my sisters. The crimson berries glistened in the first rays of sun that shone into her little kitchen. We sweated under our pinafores. A while after we put the tins in the oven, a bittersweet smell spread throughout the room.

My sister's husband had already set off with Erwin at dawn to put the last of the furniture in our new apartment. Once the cake was ready, we too hurried across the street to our apartment with brimming plates piled on our forearms.

The chilly church was packed down to the last row and filled with a delicate fragrance of flowers. Our neighbours, sitting in the pews dressed in their finest, rested their eyes on Erwin and me. For a moment I felt uncomfortable that we had only invited our closest relatives to the celebration. But how could we have accommodated and fed more people?

I trained my eyes on the minister, the father of our present one, who stood before the altar and looked far taller than Erwin. I barely recall what he said. As at every village wedding, he will have asked if I would stand by Erwin, in good times as in bad. When he stepped over to wed us, I saw that Erwin was half a head taller than him.

We didn't dance that day – fortunately, because I would have stepped on Erwin's feet. Anyway, it's not about fun, is it? We had lovely coffee and cake, a quiet afternoon, and in the evening I washed the dishes with my sister and carried the plates back to her apartment.

At Hans's wedding, Margret's parents hired a hall with a stage and wine-red satin curtains. To the clamour of brass band music the students shouted over each other instead of talking normally. My head hurt. Had I travelled a hundred kilometres for this? Erwin went from table to table in his borrowed wheelchair, but I stayed in my seat and would gladly have covered my ears. A few people came to me in turn: Hans, Margret's father in an elegant suit, skinny Margret and her even skinnier sister brought me a fresh piece of cake or a cup of coffee from the buffet and spoke for a few minutes.

A friendly man, this philosopher. His wife, like me, didn't enter the dance floor, but rather stayed seated alone at her table. Margret on the other hand danced without pause; the hem of her wedding dress lifted and fluttered, and strands of her blonde hair stuck to her temples as she spun across the floor with the students. My Hans leaned smiling against the wall, but I noticed his furrowed brow. As his smile faded, he looked as though he would happily have taken his girl by the arm and led her outside, to walk alone with her or read her a book. That's Hans, a gentleman. I would have understood if he had left with her, although he would have flouted the rules of etiquette.

Perhaps with another girl he might have returned to the village. Then in the evening he would have watched television with Erwin and could have done the man's work for me. Were he to live here, he would no longer need to lead the goats to pasture but could help the butcher check the meat or lend the doctor a hand in his surgery; meanwhile, I would dig over the beds, hoe and rake, pick vegetables and tend my flowers, some of which every second day I would tie in a posy to take to Erwin's grave. And in the evening I would cook for us.

જ

The four of them came to Erwin's funeral. Sonja kept quiet, but when the minister spoke the baby cried and the neighbours scowled at us. I would have given the wee boy the bottle, or a rag to suck, but Margret silently left with the two children. Afterwards, Hans had words with her, and I thought: you wait, girl – when your father dies, we'll do the same.

Hans was in a bad way after the funeral, held back the tears, didn't say a thing, hardly even had the strength to say goodbye to the minister – whom he knew well from before – and trembled when he offered him his hand. Minister Bauer has always looked after us selflessly, given me courage, spoken of the power of faith that could cure even the rarest of illnesses and alleviate Erwin's pain. Each week he would bring round medicine for Erwin and invite us to parish evenings, even after Hans – who might have been fourteen or fifteen years old – refused for months to go to church. I didn't know why; previously Hans had always gone willingly with me to intercession. To reassure me, Minister Bauer waved it aside, saying it was a moody phase of youth, just like Hans's infatuation with the ideas of socialism which, he said, would fade a few years after his *Jugendweihe*.

Minister Bauer was rumoured to have close relatives in the West and to want to settle over there. Erwin once said he thought the minister had three faces: one he showed people when he sat with them in their front rooms, one for the men from State Security[1], and a third that you could only guess at and which resembled the face of a great wicked wizard in fairy tales. I cared not; I like him today as I did before, although I wouldn't go to the West. Besides, Minister Bauer is still with us, leads his intercessions and finds a friendly and comforting word for everyone in the village.

At the funeral he spoke at length about Erwin's illness. The neighbours wore knitted black scarves tied around their heads, as did I.

It was March and still chilly, and I felt nothing as I thought back. But over recent months I have felt a growing bitterness, and have written several letters to the doctors who treated Erwin.

It was very hot, the summer that the village doctor referred us to the city mental hospital. For weeks Erwin had repeatedly felt strange spasms in his legs which within minutes increased and finally turned to convulsions. In vain he tried to control his muscles. I was furious, thought he was playing a joke on me, but then I saw he really was helpless. I massaged his legs from his toes to his thighs, and Erwin shut his eyes and said he thought they were settling down under the pressure of my hands. But only an hour later his feet tapped nervously on the floor, and he thumped his calves with a shrug. I was angry at him because he didn't want to see a doctor, and I made my way to the village doctor to tell him he must quickly look in.

A month later Erwin and I got out of the train in the city. I had sent Hans to my sister and packed Erwin a case that he rested on repeatedly on the way to the clinic. I gave him my arm so that he didn't fall over, because he walked on unsteady legs and the sweat was dripping into his eyes; the case I carried in my other hand.

We had made an appointment with the doctor for the following week, but I made Erwin go sooner. As he walked into the consulting room, the doctor watched him with a rigid face, and after he had shut the door behind us said, "You lied; you can walk perfectly well."

Erwin collapsed in exhaustion on the seat next to the desk. The doctor rubbed his chin with his right thumb and forefinger and said coolly, "Sorry, we have no places free until next week."

Before I could reply he reached out his arms, lifted Erwin from the chair and ushered us out the door.

Hardly were we over the threshold of our front door than Erwin's legs gave way. Each time I lifted him up he helplessly collapsed again.

I hurried to the village doctor, who sent us two nurses, and they took Erwin back to the clinic.

When I visited him a week later, I sat on the cold wooden chair between his bed and the next man's. "The first day, they gave me an injection in each leg," Erwin told me. "The spasms and the stabbing went away, and my muscles relaxed. A very nice, almost pleasant feeling. When I went to go to the bathroom I collapsed again, like at home. Right, I thought, let them bring me a urine bottle, then in a few hours I'll go over again by myself to the washrooms. But my legs remain lifeless, despite the red and white pills I've been taking morning, noon and night." He gave a sigh and said quietly, "The doctor says it's a case of a manufacturing defect."

I told Erwin that surely they would find the right drug for him; that, after all, we no longer live like we did two hundred years ago, whereupon Erwin smiled and said that he thought the same.

From then on I visited Erwin once a month. I hadn't the money to visit more regularly. Although children were allowed to visit, I took Hans only occasionally.

The man in the bed beside Erwin would start to whimper at regular intervals. Gradually his whimpers turned to shouts that merged into snarling yells; afterwards, he would press his lips tightly together, so that all you saw was a very thin reddish line. He never spoke. The hospital staff ordered Erwin not to keep laces, string, thread or rope in the room. The man had previously worked as a circus artist and frequently performed a stunt whereby he would hang from a trapeze with his wife swinging underneath, suspended from his teeth. During one of their first performances after the war, a boy in the second row took a bite from a bit of bread and ham. The smell of ham must have reached the acrobat. Inside a fraction of a second the audience's attention shifted from the ham roll to the woman, who came crashing down in the middle of the ring.

Erwin was given a wheelchair in which he would go along the hospital corridor. Sometimes we met a man with a neatly trimmed handlebar moustache, who scarcely glanced at me but stared fixedly at Erwin. Usually I pushed the wheelchair past as fast as possible. One day I was unable to avoid him because he was walking down the middle of the narrow corridor. He stopped a metre from Erwin's wheelchair, nodded first to me then to Erwin, raised his forearm into a vertical position and flapped his hand as though trying to toss it over his own shoulder. Then he extended his arm and pointed at Erwin's chest. "Destroy!" he yelled, rolling the 'r'. "With cripples like you we'll lose the war!"

Erwin reached as far forwards as he could and brusquely grabbed the man's forearm. "It was because of idiots like you that the war started in the first place!"

౮

On my sixth or seventh visit I met the doctor treating Erwin in the corridor. He said as he passed that they had found a grenade fragment in Erwin's leg and would be taking my husband for surgery. Erwin chuckled when I went up to his bed.

He was to be operated on three days later. My sister gave me some money so that I could go to the hospital the day following the procedure. On the journey Hans swung his legs incessantly and asked excitedly if Erwin would be home again soon. That morning he had fetched his ball from the shed and placed it on the faint line between the washing poles.

After knocking twice on the ward door I smiled encouragingly at Hans, who then hammered another time on the door. Without waiting for an answer we entered the room at the very moment Erwin banged his fist on the bedside table, making the crockery rattle. "I want to go home," boomed my husband's voice. I gave a start, and a young doctor I hadn't seen before took advantage of our entry to scurry through the still-open door.

"The shadow of one of my braces on the X-ray," Erwin said flatly after a time, and pounded his thighs with his fists. "Not a grenade fragment." Then he asked softly, "Take me with you?"

I nodded, not as eagerly as Hans, and told him I would see to a car.

૪૦

A few weeks later a neighbour presented me with the villagers' donation for Erwin's buggy, which he drove to the glassworks over the following weeks. Since returning from the war he no longer poured scorn on factory work, instead often saying that now we needed more of everything, especially pill bottles and test tubes. After Erwin started working there, I went to my father to help him on the farm and with the work in the field because I wanted to raise Hans at home, not at *kindergarten*†. For wages my father gave us potatoes, which we stored for the winter, and wheat, which we took to the thresher. The dust stung Hans's eyes, but we couldn't do without the flour that we carried home in sacks.

Once Hans started school I started my job at the plant. The men from the mine took no notice of my clean wet floor. As they walked down the long corridor to the dinner hall they seemed only to think of their food – cabbage soup or roast potatoes – and their cold beer. After their meal they would clomp over my now-dry floor, onto which powdery dust or tiny rock particles fell afresh, and from one of the adjacent offices I would watch as they trudged back to the entrance minute by minute in threes or fours. It didn't matter if afterwards I cleaned the bathtubs or the showers, the changing rooms or the floor, because in the afternoon or evening they would invariably enter through this same door, walk down the same corridor to eat, wash or shower, before heading home in clean clothes.

Like me, they worked in shifts. When I worked mornings, in the afternoons I would go with Hans to my father's farm. As I fetched a pail from the stall I explained the milking to him, and he kneeled in the grass with his head against the goat's belly and stroked its fur. When I put the pail beneath the udder, Hans stood up. He watched my hands, which I made alternately into fists, and began to bite his fingernails and shift from one foot to the other. I pulled his fingers away from his mouth and guided them onto the goat's udder. The goat bleated, either because her udder was still half full or because she had sensed the change. Hans withdrew his hands, folded them behind his back and stared at the milky froth in the pail. I told him that soon he would have to do it himself because sometimes I had to stay at the plant in the afternoon, too, and the goat would run away if we didn't milk her regularly. Hans looked at me in fright and unfolded his hands. I guided them a second time to the udder, closed them round the teats and repeated that he had to squeeze hard, first with his left hand then his right. As he started to milk, the goat bleated loudly, broke free and ran away across the farmyard towards the stall. Hans cried, while angrily I shook my head and pushed the pail aside so that his tears didn't mix with the precious milk.

In the days that followed he tried the milking again. Gradually it went better and the goat quietened down, but Hans took over half an hour to squeeze the last drops of milk from the udder. He could not be convinced to stop sooner. It was just the same with the other jobs. In the end my father employed a helper for the days I worked afternoons at the plant.

❧

A few years later – by now in the *Konsum* we got various sorts of meat for our marks – my father suddenly announced that he didn't want to keep his farm and field. For a while now, Hans and I had been less and less able to help him. Erwin's paralysis had spread to his waist. His buggy stayed outside our house because it was too wide for our hall and door.

My sisters' husbands didn't want to leave their self-built houses. "So you take the goat and the rabbits," my father said to me. "The hens I'll have killed, and the field I'll bequeath to my neighbour."

Behind the shed Hans nailed together from planks a small stall in which the goat lay for days, even though Hans petted her more than before. Every day he would pour a little water over her mouth, and, contrary to expectation, she lapped it up. Fearing the goat would starve, after several days Hans led her to the meadow in front of the stall. She stood motionless. Hans stroked her back and left her untethered with food at her feet. When he returned half an hour later, she had run off.

Two days after that my father had the goat killed. Hans stayed away from the feast.

∞

A few days before Erwin's death, I killed the last rabbit, a small black one that really should have grown awhile. The animal provided little meat, but I told myself it would be enough for a meal. Erwin lay motionless in bed, emaciated, numbed with painkillers, and I feared he would have no appetite. But he turned his head and smiled when I brought the tray into the room.

"How good that smells," he said softly.

I placed the tray on his bedside table, gently lifted his head and folded the pillow underneath. With a fork I carefully freed a strip of meat from the rabbit's leg, dipped it in buttermilk sauce and put the fork to Erwin's mouth. He chewed slowly, gazing at the wall, and, although he didn't say whether it tasted nice, he ate every morsel of meat then dumpling that I offered him.

The village doctor, who now came every day to monitor Erwin's drug intake and dosages, brought me a bedpan, various measuring devices, syringes and disinfectants. Erwin's skin was blistered from lying motionless on his bed, the flesh around the pressure points putrid and raw. I tended his wounds, sterilised them countless times, but when his intestinal wall ruptured and he refused to go to the clinic, within a short time pathogens infected his blood.

Finally I gave the village doctor instructions to send Hans a telegram or phone him. A few hours later he was sitting beside Erwin on one side of our double bed. I sat on the other, and thus we remained until the following morning, when Erwin died.

∞

The sun is high now, but the forest casts shadows. A clear September sky stretches above me. All of a sudden, I feel as though I would like to sit a little longer by Erwin's grave. My neighbour rarely knocks at my door, and my autumn flowers only need covering later. As it is too early for the heating, I can take care of the wood tomorrow. And the sausage for Hans? After the funeral he didn't stay at home long. In the evening I stood below on the stairs and listened as he and Margret argued in the top room. Margret's voice sounded shrill, and I thought angrily of the children asleep in the same room.

They left the next day. Although Margret politely gave me her hand in goodbye, I sensed she was relieved. When she reminded Sonja to also shake my hand, Sonja sped off like a boy. Margret called her back, but didn't tell her off a second time. If she isn't stricter with her pupils she'll have it hard.

Hans said he would write. No word about when they'll next come to visit. So I'll walk down the familiar path home and read his long letters once more, one by one, then think over his words, take up a ball of wool and start to knit the hat for Sonja so it's finished for winter.

Sleeping in the Snow

Margret • 1978

It snowed again in the early morning. As Margret parted the bathroom curtains, she saw that the snowflakes neither floated nor swirled but fell steadily in the darkness. She put on her white dressing gown and opened the door for Hans.

In the kitchen she turned on the light, cruelly announcing the day's beginning. A nauseous feeling crept up her nape to the back of her head. The short nights left their mark. In the evenings, once the children were in bed, Margret diligently prepared her lessons then took Sonja's jotters from her packed satchel, spread them on her desk and carefully checked the answers to the homework her daughter had done at after-school club. From the living room came the sound of a newscaster's voice then actors' dialogue, the rumble and roar of vehicles, shouts, screams, laughter, whines and chants. Margret blocked her ears with wax balls. Later she hung up the washing and brewed coffee for the following day.

Now, supporting herself on the sideboard she pressed the thermos flask against her forearm, unscrewed the lid and poured coffee into Hans's mug. Then she opened the fridge, placed a small bottle of condensed milk next to it, sat on the kitchen stool, poured coffee into her own mug and took a few sips.

She gazed out of the window, entranced by the snowflakes that now did dance a little. In the past she had let herself be spun around without taking her eyes from her dance partner, turning faster and faster until she became dizzy, reeled over to a chair and sat out a round, before another young man came up and offered her his arm.

Years had passed since then, and, equally, years would go by until she again had the time to dance. Would she still be able to go out in the evening? Or would she be too weak and tired? Would she prefer to once more read books that were not on the curriculum? Sometimes in bed at night Hans immersed himself in his reference books, extensive volumes with small print and sketch-like illustrations. When Margret went to bed she turned her face to the wall, away from the dazzle of his bedside lamp, and fell asleep at once.

Hans came into the kitchen. He gave off a faint smell of toothpaste and soap; his hair was smooth and neatly parted, and Margret remembered that the plain sponge cake she had bought him for breakfast a while ago was still in the fridge. She cut a piece, placed it on a small plate and slid it over to him as he stood at the sideboard drinking his coffee. Unlike before, he was now somewhat portly; Hans had never been particularly athletic, but now he needed to button his fly below his paunch.

Margret loaded a tray with bread, butter, a jar of strawberry jam, cocoa powder, plates and cutlery, and squeezed past him out of the kitchen. In the living room she set breakfast for the children, as outside in the falling snow the soldiers stamped on their morning rounds. The sound was as familiar to Margret as the ringing of the tram in front of their building. She opened the children's door; the hall light shone onto Sebastian's bed. Because he was asleep, half turned to the wall with his face partly buried in the sheets, Margret could only make out his short dark hair, flattened this way and that at the back of his head. Sonja's face, framed by her dark-blonde hair, looked peaceful and serene in the half-dark. Margret turned on their bedroom light, whereupon Sonja grimaced; soon after, she opened her eyes, squirmed, stretched her slender arms and sat up. She jumped out of bed, pulled her nightdress over her head, threw it with a flourish onto the bed end and slipped swiftly and smartly into her clothes.

Margret leaned over Sebastian's head and smelled his child's sweat, and whispered in his ear that he had to get up. She saw his eyelids stuck with sleep and stroked his warm red cheeks. He turned on his side and pulled the bedclothes up to his chin. Margret reached under the cover and shook his skinny shoulder. When Sebastian didn't stir, she gripped harder to roll him onto his back. Sebastian tensed his body, still without speaking.

In five minutes, at around half-past six, Hans had to leave the house; if Margret didn't leave with Sebastian for *kindergarten* in quarter of an hour she would be late for class. She heard her heart thumping, a throbbing in her throat and temples, then the dull metallic click as the apartment door shut. Panic seized her as she tried to recall how her mother had acted in such a situation. She could only remember Rosa's face, her kindly, grown-up expression, which Margret had dumbly obeyed.

"If you don't get up now," Margret said sharply, "I'll phone the children's home!"

Sebastian's sudden sobbing both startled and relieved her. Slowly he crawled out from under the covers and staggered into the living room.

As Margret went along the hall to the bedroom, through the open living room door she sensed the solemn gaze of her daughter, who had already eaten her slice of buttered bread and was spooning cocoa powder into Sebastian's cup of milk. Shortly afterwards Margret, now dressed, came to clear away the breakfast and saw Sonja hastily sweep up some she had spilled.

ଓ

Margret hurried across the school playground to the main entrance, where two pupils were waiting. Shoulders hunched against the cold, they shifted from one foot to the other. As the second bell rang Margret opened the school door, let in the two boys, led them to the janitor's small, stuffy room and asked him to close the door again. The main door was normally only opened to late pupils a quarter of an hour after the first bell. Now the two boys would have to wait ten more minutes with the janitor, alongside tall stacks of boxes containing the bottles of strawberry, chocolate and vanilla milk that were given out in class every day, and amongst broken broom handles, legless tables and chairs and scattered tools; after ten minutes, the janitor would go with them to their classrooms where their teacher would note their lateness in the class register.

The pupils stood up as soon as Margret shut the classroom door behind her. One girl left her place, came forward and stood several metres from her teacher before the unfolded dark-green chalkboard. The girl glanced at the front rows of benches, where some pupils sat motionless whilst others whispered or impatiently swung their feet. Then she turned to Margret and raised her hand vertically above her head. "Frau Gräf, I report that Class 6b is ready for lessons."

Margret likewise raised her hand above her head, so that the tip of her thumb touched her hair, and turned to the class. "Be prepared!"

"Always prepared!" echoed back in chorus.

The pupils sat down. Some, keen to seem inconspicuous, took from their satchels a jotter or a book and placed it at the top edge of their desk.

Margret asked if they had all done their homework. Several children lowered their heads, curled the edges of their coloured jotter covers or reached for a pencil to roll between their fingers.

"Who hasn't read the story of Kiki*?" Margret asked, prepared to excuse those who confessed.

No one raised their hand. Margret thought calmly that in the course of the lesson she would discover who was telling the truth.

She began with the lesson's theme. "Which of you has a pet?"

Several pupils raised their hands at once.

"A dwarf rabbit!"

"Two guinea pigs... Abyssinian guinea pigs!"

"A brown mouse!"

"A parrot – he's blue and yellow and green!"

"And a cat or a dog?" Margret asked.

Pupil after pupil shook their heads. "My mum says we haven't room for a dog in our apartment. A dog needs a garden and a kennel."

"My parents said that too."

"Does Kiki need a garden?" Margret asked next, looking at a girl in the front row and confidently saying her name.

The girl turned red and avoided Margret's gaze.

"Have you read the story?"

The girl answered with a faint shake of her head. Margret opened the class register to note down her name. Even though this girl rarely forgot her homework, she could no longer score top marks for effort in her half-term report card.

"Kiki lives in a barrack," another girl answered.

"And where is this barrack?" Margret continued.

"At the Spanish Inter... Interbrigades," the same girl replied. She appeared not to know the meaning of the word.

Margret asked the pupils to open their reading books. She told them that this barrack belonged to a prison camp, which in those days was on the edge of the Pyrenees, a mountain range between France and Spain; that these were two capitalist countries in southwest Europe, and that in Spain the fascists had ruled until recently. She explained that at the time of the story there had been a war between the fascists

97

and the antifascists, and lots of people from all over had helped the Spanish antifascists in the International Brigades. "For doing this, they were taken to camps, where they had to work for the fascists. At one such camp their dog lived too… And why did he have to die?"

"The prisoners were hungry and killed him," a boy said, neither quietly nor loudly, but in a voice clearly audible to Margret, who was standing behind her desk and leaning on it with her hands. For a moment she saw her father before her, which caused her thoughts to stray and made it difficult for her to react. She stared at the boy; he stared back. The room was silent, the pupils apparently holding their breaths. The boy remained straight-faced, and held Margret's gaze; he gave no clue as to how she should interpret his behaviour. She needed to act, before the corner of his mouth began to tremble; otherwise, some of the children would start laughing.

Margret remembered that the boy's grandfather, a friend of her father's, had been a professor of mathematics. Two years ago he had been dismissed from the university, whereupon he had gone to the West. The remaining family lived, unlike most pupils, in a detached house on the hillside. The boy, who continued to regard her in expectation and defiance, looked surprisingly like his grandfather.

"You will explain what you mean at the next Pioneer meeting," said Margret calmly.

Only now did the boy lower his head, merely to raise it again seconds later. "Your father is a pig," he said in a clear voice, and unhurriedly put his book and jotter in his satchel. He left the room followed by the stares of the other pupils, who sat in silence as he made his way out.

Margret's legs were shaking. She sat on her chair and mechanically asked a second time in a clear, controlled voice why Kiki had to die. Some of the pupils stared at her, while others rocked restlessly on their chairs.

"The fascists killed him," replied the girl in the front row who had not read the story.

Taken aback, Margret nodded and sighed with relief at the right answer, which nonetheless struck her as false.

※

The party meeting, which always took place in the staff room, was supposed to finish at half-past three. Nervously Margret glanced at her watch. She was sitting by the window and for half an hour had watched the party secretary, who read without pause from his paper. The chairs were set out in a horseshoe; between both ends was a table, behind which this tall man was striving to stay upright by constantly correcting his shoulders when they involuntarily sank.

Margret readily recognised the words underlined on the page, which he sought to emphasise by quickening his voice then letting it fall away again. Although younger than Margret, he spoke woodenly about the young in words he must have heard from the white-haired men in the *Politbüro*[†]. Margret knew these words meant nothing to the pupils. They came to school, joined first the Pioneers then the Free German Youth[†] and, when asked why, glanced up either in boredom or surprise and held their heads slightly awry, as though to say, "Is there any other option?" Most of them did not appear to have any career aspirations, and shrugged whenever Margret asked them about it. Initially she was surprised by their indifference. Later it alarmed her.

One day on the street she had met a ten-year-old pupil and her mother. After walking past, she heard the daughter quietly say, "Recently she asked me what I wanted to be when I was older. Of course, I didn't tell her."

But if during a lesson Margret happened to tell them about her time at boarding school, sometimes a pupil would raise their hand and suggest that their class, too, could swim in the pond in summer or autumn, or gather mushrooms; and if Margret managed to bring to life a story about children their age, alive today either here or elsewhere, sometimes they even broke into animated discussion. Now and then with older classes she noticed how a single pupil, affected by the sparing words of a poem, withdrew into themselves, a reaction she had also seen several times before in the boy who had left the class that morning.

Margret would have liked to tell someone about the incident. With some of her female colleagues she compared notes about their children, but they never spoke about their parents. Because Margret's father was known in the city, the women would probably not speak directly with her but advise her to go to the headmaster.

On occasion, Margret took it upon herself to visit her parents. A while ago, her mother had said her father had grown even more resolute and implacable in his judgment of his fellow countrymen and women: "Whoever does not stand with us must go. To reap the benefits here, and at the same time ingratiate oneself over there – that's not on."

Perhaps she should speak with the boy herself.

The party secretary read out the last sentence. It was quarter to four.

∞

In her mind Margret urged the tram driver to go faster. She knew Sebastian grew anxious from previous occasions when she had been late. She visualised him discreetly trying to get close enough to the *kindergarten* teacher to see her watch; then, he would find himself a vantage point at the door or by a window and not leave until Margret came into view. From time to time the teacher would try to draw him away – a chance for Sebastian to sneak a look at the minutes elapsed.

When she arrived, Sebastian was sitting on a stool in a corner of the group room with teary eyes. Seeing Margret, he placed his hands on the seat, ready to jump up.

"The silly-billy stood at the window for more than a quarter of an hour and didn't budge. We wanted to play a group game, but he wouldn't join us," the *kindergarten* teacher said, spreading her hands. "I tried…"

Margret understood her. The children had to learn to fit in, just as they would at school. Nevertheless, she felt sorry for Sebastian. It was her fault he had had to wait. Although she told him that now and then she might be later, he had a set time of day fixed in his head.

Margret stayed by the door while the sturdy-looking teacher paused the game, went over to Sebastian and stood in front of his stool. "You can go now," she said to him.

Sebastian slipped from the stool, ran to Margret and hugged her legs. "Tomorrow we're going to Oma's, aren't we?" he whispered, looking up at her. "And you won't have to go to school."

"Yes." Margret helped him tie his shoelaces, handed him his hat and wrapped his dark-blue knitted scarf round his neck. Then he slipped his hand in hers, and they left.

∞

"Is Sonja home?" Sebastian asked on the way home. Margret nodded and automatically walked a little faster. It often worried her that Sonja walked home alone from school, imagining she could slip on some ice, fail to see the barrier gate at the railway crossing or go with a stranger.

Home, Sebastian raced to his sister. While the two played in their room, Margret climbed onto a chair in the bedroom, lifted down the canvas suitcases from on top of the wardrobe, carried them one by one into the bathroom and beat out over the bath the thin layer of dust on each. She had to pack the cases before dinner, when Hans came home, so that there was no stress when the children went to bed and things could run smoothly the next morning. Margret had asked for a holiday on the Saturday both at her and Sonja's school, to save the children a hurried start and so as not to jeopardise their journey; when it snowed heavily the trains and buses rarely ran on time.

From the village bus stop you could reach Lene's house by either a road or a well-worn path. Margret trudged ahead, taking small steps through a virgin-white layer of snow that was ankle-deep, along the fences of the extensive gardens. It was the shorter of the two routes. Village snow, she thought, as she slipped off her gloves and reached for a handful of it, then slowly withdrew it and watched the coruscating crystals melt. Before them lay the forest, still and story-like. Margret turned round. Hans was treading in her footprints and going on and on about the road that would definitely have been ploughed, as it was every year, and where you could, unlike here, comfortably put one foot in front of the other.

His soft, dark-brown shapka on his head, Hans flexed his arms as he grumpily dragged the two cases across the snow, followed by Sebastian, who was whining because his feet were frozen. Sebastian had on the colourful striped bobble hat that Lene had knitted for Sonja a few years ago. Sonja, in a bright-red anorak with a hood that completely covered her hair, silently lifted her right then left leg in turn. Every now and then, she tottered.

The air smelled more of coal stoves than in the city. From time to time Margret looked to the snow-clad slate houses at the garden ends, where at windows, through curtains briefly parted, she made out women's faces – indistinguishable from afar, with similar-looking noses, foreheads, mouths and eyes. The faces vanished as soon as Margret looked in their direction.

Arriving at Lene's garden, Margret opened the hip-high wooden gate attached to a fence post by a loop of rope and a rusty bolt. Still free from frost, the bolt slid back easily.

Lene had shovelled a path down to the front door and spread it with salt. As they walked towards the house, a thin tabby cat ran ahead and disappeared behind the outhouse, the former rabbit hutch.

"Is that Lene's?" cried Sonja excitedly.

"Ours was black," Hans replied promptly, quietly.

They went into the dark hall. Only once they were in the living-room-cum-kitchen, and Lene had asked them to shut the door quickly, was it as warm as in their city apartment. As on every visit there was the smell of food, on the cooker a pan with steam steadily rising. The room looked unchanged. On the wooden table at the wall, spread with a brown-and-white patterned tablecloth, were a floured rolling pin, a yellowish lump of dough on a big chopping board and a long kitchen knife, placed neatly side by side. Under the table (which was used for kneading dough or scrubbing potatoes but never for eating at) were the washing-up basins that swivelled out. The dinner table in the middle of the room, however, was clean and empty because it was only set at mealtimes. Only Erwin had sometimes kneaded and rolled dough on it; Lene would push him on a chair up to the table where he would sit with his wasted legs.

Hans laid an awkward hand on his mother's shoulder and turned his head aside as their soft bellies pressed together. Lene's nose brushed his neck. Margret shook Lene's hand. The children looked up at their mother as Lene bent down, put an arm around their shoulders and drew them to her. The expression on their faces was inscrutable. Sebastian spread his arms and put his hands on Lene's thighs; Sonja's arms hung limply.

After the children had taken off their anoraks and shoes and slipped off their wet stockings, Margret opened a case and took out fresh woollen socks for them.

"Mine too," growled Hans; and Margret, who had already closed the case, opened it again. Hans sat down on the sofa, and she handed him the socks Lene had knitted whilst the children stood waiting on the linoleum in bare feet. "They fit like a glove, Mother," Hans said.

"Good, Hans," replied Lene, and robustly slid a chair over to the dinner table so that its back hit the table top. Lene gave a start then muttered dismissively, "Don't anyone sit there." Then she stooped, opened the black flap below the oven hotplate and one by one brought out warmed pairs of grey felt house shoes and sat them on the floor. The biggest pair she slid under the table to Hans. "Those were Erwin's," she said, and turned to the tall blue enamel pot on the cooker.

∞

Lene carried the pot to the dinner table and ladled chunks of stewed meat out of the soup into a shallow white dish. Margret gazed at the viscous mass in the pot, then at the chunks of meat with lumps of fat that Lene forked onto each plate.

"I'm not eating that!" Sonja said, and screwed up her mouth.

Lene looked up in shock. "That's good meat, girl," she said.

Margret was perspiring. Without a word she cut off the fat from her own meat and slipped it onto Hans's soup plate. Hans had already begun to eat, and guzzled the piece of fat without looking up.

"Your daddy always ate everything I made for him," Lene said to Sonja.

Hans didn't flinch, and kept his head lowered.

From the side, Sonja surveyed his face bowed over the plate and said with a shrug, "But I don't like it."

Margret was glad when Lene got up and opened a window. She felt damp under her armpits. She found the room cramped and stuffy, and never quite free from the smell of food; in the kitchen area cluttered with furniture and utensils she could neither stretch out her legs nor push back her chair without brushing someone else's feet or knocking something. She would have happily got up and taken a walk in the nearby snowy forest.

When Margret slipped the fourth lump of fat onto Hans's plate, Hans skewered it and held it in front of Sonja's nose.

"You will eat this now!" he said loudly.

Sonja shook her head, climbed quickly over the back of the sofa, grabbed her anorak from the wardrobe and ran from the kitchen. The coat hanger was left discarded on the floor. Margret grabbed her own coat and ran after her daughter.

Outside, Margret breathed in the chill air. It revived her, despite the smell of lignite. She spread her arms, took several strides and would have liked to shout at the top of her voice.

Close to her, Sonja was rolling a snowball ever bigger. "Look, mummy, I'm building a snowman for Sebastian!" she cried brightly, and her voice echoed and echoed.

∞

"I want a bath," Sonja said when she came into the house hours later and took off her soaking trousers.

"Then we'd have to heat lots of kettles," Margret replied. "That would take a long, long time."

"Then just a warm bed," said Sonja.

"You'll have that later," Margret told her.

After supper she asked which of the children wanted to sleep downstairs beside Oma. Sebastian stared at the floor; Sonja shook her head.

"OK then, I'll sleep beside Lene," said Margret, "and you two will let me have a lie-in tomorrow. Deal?"

The children nodded and ran ahead up the stairs to the top room, which contained a little wooden table, a chair and wardrobe, one double and one narrow single bed. At night they draped a thin woollen blanket over the window – more of a hole – onto the street. Lene had lit the stove, and the room was cosy and warm. Sebastian and Sonja whispered and laughed like two accomplices. Margret smiled when she thought of how, every night, Sebastian yawned and promised to stay awake until Sonja went to sleep. She watched as Sonja helped her brother into his pyjamas; then both children crawled into the double bed under the duvets and cried boisterously for Margret to turn off the light.

Two hours later, Margret went up with Hans to fetch her nightdress and stumbled over a pillow thrown on the floor. Brother and sister were asleep, turned towards each other under one skewed duvet, their heads nestled together. Margret found the second pillow in a corner next to the stove in which the last embers had died.

∞

Downstairs in the stoveless bedroom, both women turned their backs as they undressed. Margret knew that Lene could see her head and back in the three-way dresser mirror, and when she got up from the bed edge to remove her trousers, Lene would also be able to see her buttocks, underwear and thighs.

Lene never wore trousers. Margret was aware of her mother-in-law's movements behind her, heard the soft swish of her clothes as they brushed her skin. Lene had removed her bra and pulled her nightdress over her head, and would now slip off her skirt and petticoat. When she got up from the edge of her mattress where Erwin had previously slept, it bounced a little.

Forced to undress in the presence of another woman whom she had known some time without growing close to, Margret forced herself to stay calm. She would not undress too quickly, nor would she scatter her clothes in haste. As she gathered up her things and piled them on a chair, the biggest garments on top, she glanced at Lene, who was standing before the mirror in a heavy cotton long-sleeved nightdress, removing small silver pins from her hair. Lene's thick grey hair tumbled down her back in soft waves. At Hans's request, Margret had cut her own hair.

She lifted the bedclothes and with surprise found the hot-water bottle that Lene had placed underneath.

"I'm putting off the light now," Lene said, without looking at her.

"Good night," Margret replied. Her own voice sounded strange. After a moment she added, "Thank you for the hot-water bottle."

Lene made no response.

In the dark room, Margret's heart began to beat faster. She turned her face to the drawn curtains but did not dare get up to open them. She tossed and turned and finally lay on her back again. She stared at the ceiling then at the picture hanging above her, almost as wide as the bed.

Margret had seen the picture once by day, when she had been looking for a cardigan for Lene in the wardrobe that stood no more than a metre from the bed end. It depicted a herd of grubby white sheep whose fleeces glowed pink in the evening sun, in front of a dense mixed forest. In the foreground sat a shepherd under a tree, his head propped against the trunk, his staff next to him. Margret recalled the shepherd's burning eyes, his razor-sharp gaze. She squeezed her eyes shut, as though the man could climb down and ominously raise his staff in the air. "The Lord is my shepherd," Marie had once said. When Margret followed her up the stairs for story time, her father had always given them both a sceptical look, but her mother had said that the Bible, too, was for education.

With time, Margret had grown certain that there was no Lord. She thought of lines from the marching song: *There are no supreme saviours / no God, no Caesar, no tribune**. The shepherd would neither redeem nor rebuke her. She laid her warm hands on her chilly cheeks. Beside her, Lene began to softly snore. In all the years they had known each other, they had only ever spoken about the children's needs: what they were to eat, where to go for a walk. Never had Margret held Lene to her, who at no time seemed in need of comfort or help. Carefully Margret turned on her side and despite the darkness made out the back of Lene's head and her hair, the tips of which brushed Margret's mattress. She could have stroked it, braided it, or pulled it.

ॐ

The door creaked. Margret stirred, heard muffled voices and let her head fall back onto the pillow. Just as sleep was about to claim her again, someone tugged the bedclothes. Lene wouldn't do something like that, Margret thought, stupefied. It was dark in the room; outside it did not yet appear to be light. Margret recognised Sebastian by his smell, reached out her arm and stroked his tousled hair. "Lie beside me," she whispered, after noting in surprise that the other side of the bed was empty. "Lie still and sleep."

"I've slept in, Mummy," Sebastian cried, and hugged her so fiercely that she instantly opened her eyes and wrenched away his hands, breathing hard. In sudden rage she got up, dragged him off the bed and shoved him before her out though the door and into the living-room-cum-kitchen, which already smelled of boiled potatoes, doubtless for the dumplings that Margret forced down every time to encourage the children to eat theirs. Sonja sat dressed and combed at the table, eating her breakfast.

Margret rushed up the stairs two at a time, propelled by a singular energy she usually lacked in the morning. She flung open the door to the top room and began to shout that for once she had wanted a lie-in, that Hans was letting his mother spoil him like a child. Hans awoke from sleep and sat up with a start. Margret watched as his shock turned to anger. He got up and turned his back to her. She pulled over the wooden chair, slumped onto it and buried her face in her hands. When she lifted her head, she noticed that the woollen blanket was dangling from the window, leaving a partial view of the street. It sounded as though Hans was quickly dressing behind her. She gazed onto the street at the fresh layer of snow that had fallen in the night, the sky clear over the next-door house. As Hans stepped between her and the window and re-secured the loose half of the blanket, Margret thought to feel the day's cold.

"There's never been an argument in this house," Hans said, incensed.

"Because your mother toed the line," Margret retorted.

Abruptly Hans rattled the back of her chair. Margret could smell his breath.

"Better than your mother, who treated her children like servants!" he hissed, then stepped round the chair and slapped her face with the palm of his hand. His shirt was only half-buttoned. His chest hairs merged into a dark fuzzy patch.

"Why did you want children anyway?" Margret muttered.

She walked to the door and heard a thud behind her as the chair crashed to the floor. Quick, to the bathroom, she thought, so the children don't see me now.

It had not occurred to Margret that in the bathroom, a small chamber beside the laundry room that stank of sewage, there was, unlike in the kitchen, no sink; but Lene and the children were in the kitchen. Margret went to the inflow tap and cooled her reddened cheek. Water sprayed her nightdress, the cold stone floor and her feet. She padded over to the dry closet, sat on the black lid and opened the little lace-curtained window. Dead flies lay on the sill. Her eyes met those of the women next door, who stood barely three metres from the garden fence and appeared to be watching her. Swiftly Margret shut the window, causing several flies to fall to the floor.

She could not go home, nor had she sufficient strength to spend a further day here. The smell of the toilet chamber made her sick, as sick as she had felt when Sonja had begun to grow in her belly, invisible to all. The children were no longer little but not yet big enough to manage without her. In her head Margret drew up the sequence of events she had to follow: get up from the toilet, dress in the bedroom, walk casually into the kitchen, greet everyone brightly, avoid argument with Hans, perhaps look at a book with Sebastian or offer Lene her help. Not think about tomorrow.

In the kitchen a few minutes later, Margret put the kettle on the cooker and shook coffee powder into a big mug. She was aware of her silent children's stolen glances and felt ashamed when she heard Hans's footsteps in the top room.

"The thin walls never bothered us," Lene said.

Margret ignored the note of rebuke in Lene's voice, poured her coffee and sat next to Sonja and Sebastian, who were both flicking through books. Every now and then Sonja looked over at Lene, who was scrubbing potatoes in a bowl with damp red hands. Sonja studied not only Lene's hand movements but also her robust body and the absorbed expression on her face as she pressed then opened her lips. Margret watched her daughter. She found it strange that Sonja should be interested in Lene and her kitchen work.

Margret had just finished her coffee when Hans came into the kitchen. He avoided her gaze, stood vacillating. Lene put down a half-scrubbed potato, shook her fingers over the bowl then dried her hands with a dishtowel. Her overall stretched across her rear as she crouched, took a mug from the lower section of the sideboard and asked Hans how many spoonfuls of coffee powder he wanted. Hans waved dismissively, and told the children that after breakfast he was going to shovel snow and would take them into the garden with him. Whereas Sonja acted as though she had not heard him, Sebastian jumped to his feet and pulled on his shoes.

"I'll go ahead with Sebastian," Margret said, and thought of the previous day, of the liberating feeling that had set in outside the house. As she rummaged in the hall for her gloves, Lene came up behind her and whispered that perhaps two children were too much for her. She held out Margret's gloves. Silently Margret turned away and clenched her fists inside her coat pockets.

Outside, with the shovel propped over her shoulder, Margret made footprints in the snow up the garden path. At the top of the garden she shovelled clear a small square area. Sebastian formed some lumpy snowballs in his mittens. Mechanically Margret threw them one after the other against a washing pole or just wide, and heard Sebastian exclaim in excitement or disappointment. She craved sleep. Her hands scarcely felt the cold of the snow. She would willingly have buried herself in it.

Suddenly the front door opened. Sonja ran out, made a snowball and threw it with all her might at Hans, who had just emerged. Margret watched as he carefully closed the door, and she wondered whether or not he suited the house. Sonja's snowball hit him on the stomach, and he kneeled. As he laid down his shapka, Sonja swiftly stuffed another snowball in his anorak hood and tipped it over his head.

"You crazy little noodle," Hans grumbled, as he brushed the snow from his head. Sonja snatched his shapka and filled it with snowballs which she then flung one after the other in Hans's direction, with Sebastian's help. Hans tried to dodge them by stumbling around over the snow-covered lawn, but the children ran up to him and pressed the last balls against his jacket until in the end all three were falling and laughing and rolling in the snow.

Margret leaned against the washing pole. She would have liked to put on her gloves. Tomorrow she would be home again. Tomorrow, she decided, she would talk to the boy who had insulted her father.

∞

On Monday the pupil entered class again just as matter-of-factly as he had left on Friday. He raised his hand like the other pupils in the Pioneer salute and sat in his seat in the third row.

During the lesson Margret occasionally glanced at him. Although he gazed out the window and did not take part in the lesson, he would probably know the right answer if she asked him a question.

After the lesson she walked up to his seat. He seemed strangely isolated; no other pupil was waiting for him, and none had said they would wait outside. Impassively he obeyed when Margret asked him to come to the front.

When they were standing face to face, the boy looked away.

"What has my father," Margret asked gently, "to do with the lesson?"

The boy shrugged silently, and Margret noticed his curved back, which made his gangly body look like a thin question mark. He had his hands buried in his pockets. Other sixth graders constantly fiddled with something or chewed their fingernails when Margret spoke to them. Most of them were timid, but this boy seemed both stubborn and fearless. And he would probably say nothing at the Pioneer meeting, even silently accept being expelled from school.

"We want to leave anyway," he blurted out suddenly, defiantly.

Margret hid her shock at his candid admission. "That would be a shame," she said.

"It doesn't matter whether you know or not. They're always watching us," the boy added.

They were silent.

"But why do you think it will be better there?" Margret asked.

The boy shook his head. "We don't. But Opa..." He fell silent and his shoulders sagged, accentuating his question-mark shape. Then he turned around and began to cry, wiping the snot with his pullover sleeves. Margret thought of Sebastian sitting on the chair at *kindergarten* with reddened eyes.

Quietly she searched her skirt pocket for a clean handkerchief but could find only a scrunched-up one. So she walked round, slid over a chair and gently pushed the boy down onto it. He did not resist. From the playground, cries and laughter drifted up from children throwing snowballs or sliding along a thin line of ice. The boy should be out there with the others, Margret thought. But she could not bring herself to send him out because she wanted to learn what had happened back then. She began again, "Your Opa and my father knew each other..."

The boy nodded faintly. "They were friends, but your father decided Opa should leave."

"Yes," Margret replied. "Friendship is not the most important thing for him. But how do you know that?"

"Heard it when my parents were arguing," said the boy.

Margret was shocked at the boy's detached tone of voice. Would Sonja or Sebastian say the same about her and Hans in a few years?

"But Opa," said the boy, "is my friend."

He dug out a handkerchief from his pocket and loudly blew his nose. The voices from the playground grew quieter and faded before echoing again a short time later in the school corridors. A girl opened the classroom door, apologised and shut it again. Margret hastily said to the boy that he need not say anything at the Pioneer meeting, that she had only wanted to ask him not to disrupt the lesson again. The boy stood up without answering. Together they went to the door, where

Margret laid her hand on his shoulder before he moved off and she lost sight of him in the throng of other children.

On the way to her next class, it struck Margret that Sonja and Sebastian rarely visited Friedrich and Johanna without her or Hans. Her father had taken Sonja for a walk a few times when she was still in her pram, but now, as soon as one of the children ran up to him and entreated him to play, he escaped to his study. Johanna occasionally read the children a story, but if they wanted to hear a second one, she grumbled that she was not their mother. Her brusque tone drove the children into the garden or one of the attic rooms, where they had set up their own collection of toys: sticks and stones and faded leaves, dried flowers, old glass and scraps of paper.

Hans's father, on the other hand, had often played with Sonja until his death. He had sewn her a rag doll, kneaded dough figures with her, from his buggy thrown her a ball that she tried to catch and ran after if she missed. It was too rough a game for a girl, Lene had said querulously at the time.

Margret brushed aside memories of their weekends in Lene's village. Lines from the poem she would discuss next lesson went through her head: *Bowed over the poppy / he eagerly tries to determine / how nature made this flower / in all its detail**. She winced; Hans had been like that when she had got to know him. A silent pain welled up inside her as she compared memories distant and near.

114

Fragile Specimens

Hans • 1981

Before Margret had left the apartment after the row, Sonja had emerged from the children's room. Her wide nightdress hung loosely on her sprouting, slender body. She had blinked under the glaring hall light and said she could not sleep. She would not let Margret take her in her arms, but instead stole soundlessly past to the bathroom like a winged creature that barely brushed the ground. Hans, caught helpless, had for the first time felt ashamed in front of her.

Whenever Hans fought with Margret he began to yell; she would whimper, his anger would grow, and the more furious he became, the louder she would cry; finally, his limbs would seem to move of their own accord: he would kick her on the shin or strike her on the face; she would briefly cry out before her cries subsided into quiet sobs. That had always been the pattern – only not today. He had hardly felt the sting on his cheek. Sudden silence set in. He had stopped moving and slumped onto the sofa behind him. Margret had gone into the hall, sent Sonja back to bed, and the front door clicked shut.

Hans stared at his thighs as the children talked quietly in the next room. Gradually he realised that only Sonja was talking. She was trying out various voices to comfort her brother: first a bright and breezy tone to cheer him up; then she growled menacingly and told him he had better stop crying or else she would go crazy; finally, her voice sounded plaintive, pleading, almost suppliant. Hans sat glued to the sofa with no idea what to say to them. After one row a few years ago, Margret had asked him why he had wanted children. He had not needed to think about it; he knew why, now as then – because children belong to a family; this was something normal and natural, unless you were a paraplegic like his father.

All the same, the children drove him to distraction with their defiance, their insolence, their dogged determination and boundless energy, and the chaos they spread around them. Day by day Hans stayed longer at the herbarium, where he was surrounded by peace and order, sighed with relief as soon as he entered his office and was loath to leave, because at home the children's room resembled a battlefield and before long the few objects that still had an obvious use were put to another: a teddy became a chair, a chair a house, a book a roof, clothes were made into curtains, paper into snowflakes or sugar. When Hans knocked on their door, Sonja and Sebastian either barricaded it, screamed, or flung it open to hug him. His head threatened to burst from their screams, and he broke out in a sweat.

One Sunday in early autumn – Margret was in the middle of helping Sonja with some difficult homework – Hans had gone with Sebastian for a walk in the forest. Sunlight streamed through the treetops as they walked to a spot where Hans knew honey fungus grew on the dead trunk of a fallen tree. The forest was fragrant with mushrooms and alliums, with last night's rain seeping up through the soil. Sebastian skipped around on the still-damp paths, collected fragments of wood, brittle bits of bark and dark-red leaves, and, when they came to the tree trunk, Hans pressed an opened pocketknife into his son's hand. Then Hans had begun to cut away the mushrooms and fill the wicker basket with them, and in the end cut them all off himself because Sebastian had settled next to the dead tree stump, absorbed in scraping the dirt from under his fingernails with the knife. He appeared not to be bored, but had no interest in either the mushrooms or the names of the trees or flowers, and Hans had felt distant from his own son; Sebastian was an alien being to him, and, although obedient most of the time, Hans did not know what went on inside his head.

All the same, Sebastian behaved differently to Sonja, who refused to answer him and constantly followed her own will. Within seconds she made him furious and was even unafraid of his raised hand, instead laughing until he hit her.

His own mother, thought Hans occasionally, would long since have established order.

∞

The children were quiet now, probably asleep. Hans remained immobile on the sofa, speculating over where Margret might have gone. He was worried something could have happened to her. Perhaps she had walked up the lighted stairway at the back of their building to the forest edge where the line of dim, dirty lights ended, and was now walking aimlessly through the dark, or else had set off purposefully along another path, although Hans could think of no one whom she could visit at eleven at night. He clasped his hands: what if she didn't come back? No, even if she left him, she would never leave the children. He tried to imagine there being another man, but was unable to.

The sound of the key turning in the lock was barely audible, but still Hans gave a start. A waft of chill damp night air seeped through from the hall, heralding the end of summer. Margret walked past the living room into the children's room. Hans remained rigid, hands freshly clasped. Soon after, Margret walked down the corridor to their bedroom, ignoring him. Although Hans did not know how he should face her from now on, he felt a load start to lift.

He waited a moment before standing up, then quietly opened the bedroom door and pulled out his pyjamas from under the bedclothes. Margret lay motionless as usual, on her side of the bed. He lay down beside her and listened to her breathing.

৪০

It was always at night, between bouts of deep sleep, dozing and wakefulness that he was beset by images. With the morning light far away, an end to his turmoil seemed impossible tonight, too.

Hans had forgotten how it felt to have his cheek smart from a slap. At first he thought it had never happened before. But then he saw himself standing in a field: dry, yellowish plants are sprouting from the ground, the dark-green forest not far off like a wall; a light wind is blowing. He does not feel cold, but his stomach rumbles. With a small hoe he loosens the earth, pulls at a plant, tears it off and throws it onto a pile beside him. Saliva collects in his mouth. He scrapes a little earth from the potato and bites into it. Behind him he hears someone breathing. He gulps down the acrid mouthful. Suddenly the potato falls from his hand, which starts to smart, as does his cheek soon after.

"That's poisonous!" his mother shouts.

Hans starts to cry in fright.

"Don't cry; there's food at home." His mother bends down again and unflaggingly pulls up potatoes. He too continues with the work. It feels as though his left cheek were mushrooming into the air. He imagines it swelling up and how he must look, as if he had stuffed a soft ball or a balloon in his mouth. His father sometimes said that when you were hungry, you fantasised.

It seemed he had only been asleep a few minutes, but he was unsure. His pyjamas stuck to his skin; he could smell his night sweats and would gladly have drifted into dreamless sleep. In the silence he pressed his hands to his ears, as though thereby to silence his thoughts; instead, they crisscrossed his mind as images: Margret's surprising physical strength, her fearless expression. He took his hands from his ears and grabbed at the air to loosen his cramped fingers. Strange that he had not struck her back. Ultimately, she was the weaker. But Hans had been taken aback, not enraged.

Now that Margret had stood up for herself, she seemed inviolable.

Hans turned on his side. The hands of the ticking clock glowed luminous green. Soon the night would be over. Whether night or day, the hours tick by, he thought without regret.

⚬

As on every morning, at half-past six Hans got into the yellow tram crammed with people, men and women his age; older and younger ones, too, with tired faces, very few awake and vocal. The tram smelled of aftershave and deodorant, bitter coffee breath, last night's alcohol. Hans gripped the cold metal of a seat-back handle and let the familiar buildings – the barracks, the small garden nursery, apartment blocks, the school, the hospital, more apartment blocks – glide by. Because he was standing in the middle of the tramcar hardly anyone came and stood beside him; most new passengers stayed close to the door. Hans enjoyed the warmth, even if he was starting to feel sick from all the smells.

Along with Hans, most people got out in the town centre. It was not far to the herbarium. As he entered his office, Hans felt neither anticipation nor relief. He sat down at his desk and looked out over the botanical gardens. To the right grew a chestnut tree with a broad crown. A chestnut dislodged itself from a branch and fell onto one of the snaking stone walls. Hans thought he heard the thud as it burst open. The brown nut rolled off the wall and a little way onto the earthy path.

He felt calmed by the greenness, the attractive and thoughtful layout of the plants, their unusual forms and colours. There were delicate shrubs from Asia with the finest of leaves and blossom in pastel shades in spring, bushes with fleshy foliage, trees with thick trunks and tiny fruit, and each of these specimens bore a label with its specific name in German and Latin, along with its country of origin.

Hans took a deep breath, in then out, and lowered his head over the three thick plant presses sent to him to have their contents identified by a Rostock University researcher, who had brought them back from a trip to Sweden. With tweezers Hans gently grasped a pressed flower as big as a man's hand and placed it on the white sheet next to it. The flower was as thin as strong paper, partly dried and dull in colour, and over the course of time it would grow increasingly fragile. Hans cut some adhesive strips and fixed the flower to the paper. To the lower right he left a space for the label.

He would learn the plant name from his classification books. He need only deliberate on days when plants arrived that did not feature in the books. Then he had to consult further volumes and, if he found no satisfactory reference there either, allocate the plant a place in the classification system. From time to time the entire system had to be renewed. On such days (as yet these had been few and far between) Hans worked together with colleagues from another institute, because his own work normally consisted of archiving. He became caught up in his dream to investigate new species, and would set about his work with particular excitement, initially enthused then later exhausted by it, so that by the end he felt renewed certainty that he had made the right decision back then.

ဆ

Once on a trip to Mexico he believed he really had discovered a new plant species. Disappointed, he later found the plant in the herbarium of the National University of Mexico City but still took it home with him, along with the countless other plants that had aroused his interest. The small avocado tree adorning his broad windowsill today had grown from a stone brought back. But the jasmine beside it, whose thin tendrils twisted upwards on a wooden trellis, he had bought in an ordinary flower shop in Switzerland.

Hans was promised the trips after he finished his studies; undecided as to his next step, he confided in a good colleague.

"Cataloguing plants, that would be the thing for you," Fred had said. "We need people for that, and it would facilitate the odd trip. You've been a comrade a long time now... Could you imagine joining the university party leadership? Have a think about it."

Hans had joined the Party as an eighteen-year-old. At that time, questions regarding the suitable microscope or the right acids, the sufficient number of glass cover slips and pipettes had seemed more important than a student's political views or background. Anyway, all students alike were allowed to conduct research analysis on the botanical and zoological specimens imported long ago from overseas, which were of particular value. Even though Hans and his fellow students rarely undertook group work in the lab, there was a certain togetherness, a common interest in the work.

One of their lecturers managed in every lecture to transport them for an hour and a half to a world of ideas from which they were reluctant to emerge; pondering his words, the students put away their notes in a leisurely fashion and poured out of the benches in silence. One day, a friend nudged Hans on the way out and said, "A great lecture, even though he's not in the Party!"

Hans nodded. Another student muttered as he passed that the majority of the lecturers and professors weren't comrades anyway.

Five years later, though, Fred had put this question to him about joining the university party leadership, and Hans had accepted. Childhood images popped into his head again: how he had laid aside the scythe to pull out separate stubborn grass blades, one of which had cut his finger; how he had clenched his teeth, and how his mother had simply said, "Go inside if you can't be of help to me here."

Hans visualised himself standing before a learned audience, sliding his finger across an overhead projector and explaining in English how plants were catalogued in his country. He pictured himself as he passed round photos amongst friends and family, looked into their amazed or inquiring faces and answered all their questions with ease. Perhaps he would even read his name in newspapers with English titles.

There was little to do on the party leadership board; he need only attend the monthly meetings, prepare a speech now and then and be an example to his colleagues. Patiently Hans would talk to them and bring up their problems for discussion with the leadership board. The right way stood open to all who wished to follow it.

∞

Hans stepped from his office into the corridor, turned right and walked over to one of numerous tall cabinets. He slid open the light grey door, took a handful of labels from a shelf and sauntered back towards his desk. A colleague was walking down the corridor. Hans greeted him with a handshake and exchanged a few words. Unpractised in talking to colleagues, he stumbled over his words and eventually said goodbye. The labels (which Hans would usually carry carefully, almost reverently, to his desk) had become damp and slightly crinkled from his thumb hold. He laid them on the table and stacked several books on top. After a few minutes he removed them, smoothed them out and in black ink wrote under the printed name of the herbarium the origin of the plant whose flower head filled the page, its species and today's date. Next to his office door was a row of cabinets containing stacked herbarium files. Though these were regularly dusted, Hans thought to detect a musty smell as he contemplated them. It was the smell of old, lifeless specimens, preserved for future generations of students and scientists; easy to find, apparently indestructible.

Suddenly Hans had the sensation of swallowing dust. Quickly he inhaled, but his mouth and lungs seemed only to fill further with dust. Nausea rose in him and he flung open the window. The botanical gardens fell away gently to the east. Down there was the entrance, where a young couple stood in an embrace. On the adjacent path students were walking, gesticulating, laughing and elbowing each other. The sun lit up the gold-green leaves of a maple tree. Some fallen leaves danced across the stone paving. Hans heard bird cries, people's voices, the noise of cars, a helicopter, a circular saw; he smelled someone nearby burning something in their garden but was not sure what it was.

Footsteps echoed not far from his open office door. The idea of going out to the corridor, addressing the person and entering into conversation seemed strange to Hans. In recent years he had seldom spoken with colleagues; it seemed pointless, futile, time lost, a distraction from work and a source of conflict.

When he was studying, Hans had been good friends with Peter, a fellow student. When collecting specimens together for botanical research they would often talk, seeking mutual exchange and friendship. Peter had painted a gloomy picture of their future. "Where'll it lead to if people are attacked for airing their thoughts?" he asked Hans. Hesitantly he named some examples. Hans firmly shook his head and refused to believe him.

When they had completed their studies, both with distinction, it was Peter who would far rather have taken up a post at the herbarium than Hans.

At a party leadership meeting Hans was told he should break off contact with Peter. Aware that it was necessary, Hans had done so with a heavy heart, and not without speaking to his friend beforehand. They were sitting on the dry summer grass, the sun shining on their bare necks.

"Are you sticking to your stance?" Hans asked.

"Yes," his friend had answered, smiling.

"All the best, then." Hans got to his feet and extended his hand to Peter, who slowly stood up.

He cried quietly on the way back. Peter did not follow him.

Hans was subsequently asked to report what he knew about Peter. Although he felt uncomfortable, he withheld nothing.

Hans heard nothing more from Peter; but on his travels he met many other people different in outlook, in their way of thinking, talking and being. He saw all kinds of landscapes: reddish rock, wide rivers with impressive bridges, skyscrapers, well-maintained centuries-old buildings, buildings with crumbling plaster.

But on every trip Hans's thoughts were of his village, and thus he forgot to take photos; his lectures became mechanical, and he talked politely to people in the knowledge that it would be some time before he met them again, if at all.

While his mother lived in a constant state of worry about him, he sampled various wines on the plane, listened to a lecture on plants (whose names and appearance she would have thought exotic), or joined a group of international researchers on an outing to a national park. Because his mother had no phone, the day Hans arrived in a foreign country he would write her a postcard which she often only received after his return. And yet, every time he visited her with Margret and the children, with a look of approval and with satisfaction in her voice she said, "You've made something of yourself. The money for your studies wasn't in vain."

She nodded thoughtfully as she said it. Hans then placed some money on the table and told her to buy a washing machine or install a bath, and his mother opened the kitchen cupboard door, slipped the notes under the blue patterned cup and shut the door again.

"On Monday I'll put it in the bank," she said, "so the children get some of it one day."

On one of his last visits to the village, Hans had felt her eyes linger on him. "Are you really only allowed these trips because of all your successful work?" she asked him. One morning several years ago, she continued, two men had stood at her door, but she had slammed it in their faces with the words: "You're not getting my son!" As she told Hans this, she sat upright with her chin held aloft.

Hans was startled, and suddenly thought to understand why in all these years he had not been recruited by State Security. Certainly he would not have refused the offer – he knew his duties; nevertheless, he was glad he had not been given the choice. He told his mother that he was involved with the university party leadership.

She nodded. It was the same nod with which she had acknowledged the sense behind the effort to pay for his small rented room, his canteen food and his exam attire. "I'm not like Minister Bauer," she said; "I've nothing against living in this half of the country." She had also been in favour of the division, she told him; after all, here poorer people's rights were protected. Others in the village had been angry because they had had to hand over property, but her family had never owned much anyway. "But these men have no place in our village," she said. "We can take care of ourselves, and we've got the minister for problems."

☙

The late afternoon sun shone softly. Hans was undecided whether to work on or go home. He had mounted and labelled all the flowers, leaves, stems and roots from the first plant press, and foregone his lunch for it. He didn't yet feel hungry. Perhaps tomorrow he would ask one of his colleagues if they wanted to eat with him in the canteen.

He could take a detour through the graveyard, which was like a silent park with gravestones hidden behind bushes and rows divided by hedges. Hans knew only a few names on the stones: one of Margret's pupils who had died in an accident, a doctor found hanged in the forest, a former colleague who had been an alcoholic. Their graves were in the upper part of the cemetery, a little way off the main paved pathway, at the sides of which grew tall chestnut trees. Perhaps over recent windy days some chestnuts would have detached, fallen onto the path and burst open. Perhaps some leaves would have blown off, still smooth and green, leaves that barely rustled as you passed.

Hans hurriedly cleared his desk and left the herbarium more punctually than usual, strangely glad about this hour he would spend neither at work nor at home.

At the graveyard entrance he decided to leave the main pathway and stroll along the smaller paths between the graves. He glanced at the gravestones and the shrubbery (which he studied like museum pieces, voyeuristically, dispassionately) as he drew near a moss-covered stone basin. He stooped over the clear water, which reflected his face. He paid scant regard to his reflection, gazing instead at the bottom of the basin where lay greenish coins, pebbles and rotting leaves, and the longer he looked down the more it seemed to him as if the basin were getting deeper and deeper, turning into a well, becoming bottomless; at last, only his face could be seen. He turned away and heard a frail male voice behind him. From the other side of the path approached Margret's father Friedrich, erect and walking briskly, even though two years ago he had suffered a heart attack and been retired ever since. Still slim, he wore an elegant suit with a neat tie. His white hair was carefully combed. Surprised to meet him here, Hans walked towards him. Friedrich transferred a small vase from his right hand to his left to greet him.

"I tend the grave of a comrade I was friendly with," Friedrich said, preempting Hans's question and briefly brandishing the vase. "And you, young man?"

"I'm taking a walk," Hans answered, and smiled wryly at Friedrich's form of address.

Friedrich went to the basin, rolled up his right sleeve to below the elbow, stepped back half a pace, stretched out his arm, dipped the vase and filled it with water.

Hans walked with him to the small unpretentious grave, left unplanted with only a rectangular stone and a small plinth. Friedrich placed the vase on top and arranged some carnations in it.

"He gave everything for our cause," said Friedrich quietly.

Hans glanced at the gravestone and gave a start, because the year of birth was his own.

"Abandoned by his wife and children," Friedrich said, "but didn't let himself be bribed – fought to the end."

With these last words, Friedrich's voice took on a rich melodious ring that reminded Hans of the village minister's voice. As though talking to a great crowd, Friedrich's gaze wandered over the graves. Then he touched Hans on the shoulder – Hans, thinking of the minister, stepped back – and said with a smile, "I won't live to see communism in its pure form. But your generation – for certain." Head lowered, Friedrich slowly rolled down his sleeve.

Hans made no answer. Of course communism would come some day; when, he did not know. He studied Friedrich, who had always seemed young to him, and for the first time noticed the dry, lined skin on his face, the brownish blotches on his hands. Hans wanted to ask how his heart was when Friedrich suddenly said, "One day the university will receive my books, so that all the others can benefit from them."

He is a generous and uncompromising man, Hans thought; then he called to mind his own books in his office, the silence of his room, and he would have liked to ask Friedrich whether the man whose grave he tended had died from an illness, or because of his loneliness, his isolation.

For a time they stood silently side by side at the grave. Then Friedrich said, "I must get home; I've an article to finish." As they shook hands, he asked hesitantly, "How are Margret and the children?"

"They're all well," Hans nodded in reply; then, releasing his father-in-law's hand, he said goodbye and hurried off towards the main pathway.

End of Waiting

Johanna • 1984

When Johanna entered the main university building, with Margret holding her right arm, she was greeted by a line of people extending from the still-shut auditorium door to the foyer. She felt Margret's grip tighten but, thanks to the pills she had taken at home an hour before, felt removed from events around her.

Slowly they approached the guests, and Johanna recognised individual people nodding to her: the university rector, Friedrich's assistants, his colleagues and students. As she reached the first of them, she pushed back her shoulder blades, looked him in the eye and impassively accepted his condolences, words with which he sought to express his regard for Friedrich's work.

Once they had reached the end of the line, the heavy wooden door opened from inside. Suddenly Johanna felt the piercing gaze of a stranger in the line of guests. Her knees went weak. Could it be that there was someone here who took satisfaction from Friedrich's death? Who had come to relish the fact that every word uttered pertained to a dead man?

She made an effort to walk faster, but her legs felt like two blocks that would barely leave the floor. Eventually she reached her seat, accompanied by Margret. Next to the huge painting at the front of the auditorium hung a black-framed photograph of Friedrich, similar in size and shape to the portrait of the head of state on the other side of the painting. She averted her eyes from Friedrich's picture opposite and gazed instead at the painting, which had become familiar to her over the years. In the foreground were students saddling their white and ruddy-brown horses, smartly slipping on their uniforms to go to the War of Independence†; far beyond, the fields shimmered in soft pastels; in between marched columns of young men shouldering rifles with bayonets.

Strange how the music that now resounded befitted the scene. Was this symphony not based upon the triumph over Napoleon, his imminent defeat? Johanna heard quiet sobbing, barely perceptible sniffles, a rush of whispers; the music now sounded solemn, now soft as spring, but never descended into outright sorrowfulness. Friedrich had admired the power of Beethoven. At home Johanna would put on the final chorus of the *St Matthew Passion*, even though Friedrich disapproved of the fact that Bach had written church commissions.

"What was he to do? He had to earn a living," she answered him time and again, whereupon Friedrich usually murmured, "He lived in the wrong time, the good chap."

After the music had faded, first to approach the microphone was the rector. His words were followed by those of one of the young assistants, who spoke of Friedrich's unshakable materialist standpoint which left no room for cowardly compromises or mistaken beliefs. Just like the natural sciences, so too history had its principles; such an attitude was imperative for a philosopher today.

Over all the years, Johanna had supported Friedrich's work – in that she had employed a reliable household help and kept the children away from him while he was working – beyond all the doubt that arose in her at regular intervals.

Johanna clearly remembered the last time she would have been glad to share her doubt with Friedrich. A neighbour had been telling her about Clara, a girl in her youngest daughter's class. Clara, freckly, mostly serious and thoughtful, frequently wore the dresses her mother had worn as a girl. The other children whispered about her. Clara acted as though she was unaware. One day the children were talking about the night when they were to be admitted to the Free German Youth: the torchlit procession, the darkness, who was going with whom; and, without any of the children asking, casually Clara said that she still needed time to find out whether God approved of her joining. The others tapped their fingers against their temples, changed the subject and talked about the films they had seen on West German television. Days later, two boys twisted Clara's arm up her back while two other girls prised open her mouth and placed several pieces of chalk on her tongue. Clara choked and spat out the bits, which fell onto the classroom floor to be trampled by some of the children into chalk dust, to which they added some plant water. They pushed Clara onto her knees and her mouth down to the white watery mush. At that moment the teacher had entered the room and the children had dispersed, leaving Clara on the floor, and the lesson had begun with the teacher's customary words.

The assistant's voice reached Johanna as if from afar. She heard him describe Friedrich's role in the antifascist resistance struggle, and again her mind strayed. "These men and I, we have a common past," Friedrich had once said to her. It had been on a 1st May, as they walked past a podium erected for the holiday, surrounded by people with paper flags fluttering in their hands. Waving children walked with them, wearing Pioneer neckerchiefs or *FDJ* shirts. On the podium stood men who looked less frail than Johanna, neither old nor young, just void of vitality, stiff like wooden puppets. Johanna had watched as now Friedrich too raised his hand. She would have liked to take it back down and hold it in hers. He, who had taken such care over his dress that morning and walked so upright beside her, appeared not to find it incomprehensible that, year after year, to the sound of drums, timpani and fanfare, thousands of people saluted some functionaries who masqueraded as representatives of the party of the working class.

For some time now Johanna had simply pinned a small red paper carnation to her jacket and refused to brandish a flag.

Her daughters seemed hardly to be breathing. None of them blew their noses. Johanna sensed them sitting paralysed beside her.

"His work has left a lasting legacy on our city's university," the lord mayor said.

Of the grandchildren, only a grown-up son of Rosa's had come; Margret's children were spending the weekend with friends and Tanya's were visiting their other grandparents.

"We thank him from the bottom of our hearts for his contribution to the formation of our socialist society," the lord mayor closed his speech.

Beyond all the doubt: again, the words went through Johanna's head. Perhaps it was good that Friedrich had died before her. She flinched at the thought. Could Friedrich not see how angry and discontented some people were, how bitter their laughter as they read the newspaper, watched television or returned from meetings? He would have warned them to stick to the party line, and they would have shaken their heads at him, or else clenched their fists. For a long time she had believed in the same thing as him, until she sensed that her hope's lifeblood had run dry. Then Johanna would have liked to be Friedrich's hope, but one person was not enough for him.

Someone touched her arm, and when she turned her head, she saw the guests were slowly pouring out into the aisle.

"We have to say goodbye," whispered Margret.

Why here, why so soon, Johanna wondered, until she understood that Margret had not meant saying goodbye to Friedrich; she had been thinking about him so much that she believed he must be standing before her and would say a few words to her.

His portrait bore a black ribbon over the lower-right corner. Johanna shivered. While Margret and Tanya held up their arms, Rosa raised Johanna from her seat.

"I don't want to," Johanna hissed, but the young assistant had already come up to her and was bowing. Tanya lifted Johanna's arm slightly, and soon after, the assistant, rector and lord mayor shook her hand in succession.

Before Johanna climbed into the taxi, again her eyes met those of the man who had caught her attention in the line of people paying their respects. A few years ago, she now remembered, this man had visited Friedrich at home, and Johanna, writing her letters on the first floor, had heard their raised voices. He was the son of a former mathematics professor who had left the country. At the time, Friedrich had said the son would probably soon follow his father.

Johanna nodded to the man, who rested his eyes on her but did not return her greeting. Then the taxi driver helped her into the passenger seat and Margret climbed into the back, while the other two daughters started their own cars.

When they arrived at the house, Johanna, supported by her daughters, climbed the narrow ramp to the front door, entered the dark hall (which still smelled faintly of pipe tobacco) and collapsed before one of her daughters could switch on the light.

She woke up on the living room sofa where Friedrich had slept in the previous weeks, while Johanna, seeking to be near him, had set herself a place to sleep on the narrow settee by the door. At first she had tried to look after him alone, but then had asked Margret and the household help. Day and night over several months, she and Friedrich had lain in the same room and were thus – for the first and last time – hardly apart.

Johanna opened wide her eyes and looked into Margret's face, which had become familiar again over recent years. Her other two daughters, however, she had scarcely recognised when they arrived at the house the day before the memorial service.

"Where are Rosa and Tanya?" Johanna asked.

"They've driven home," Margret replied. "The doctor was here. You should stay in bed for now."

Margret pulled up the woollen blanket around Johanna's neck, but Johanna pulled it back down so she could breathe more easily. She felt as though a hard board were pressing down on her ribcage; she was sweating.

"You fainted, before you fell asleep," Margret told her.

Johanna tried to turn on her side. After rolling back several times, she felt Margret's hands under her back and bottom, cold hands that determinedly rolled her onto her side and then spread the blanket over her upper body again. Johanna hit out at Margret's arms, making her daughter step back.

"I have to collect the children," Margret said. "I'll come in the evening to wash you."

"Just leave me alone," Johanna said.

"You're not alone. The household help is here," Margret replied.

∞

In the evening Johanna heard in the hall footsteps that sounded louder than Margret's. Hans came in cautiously, but still Johanna gave a start.

"Margret will come when the children are asleep," he said. He set down a grubby white warming pot on the little wheeled table beside Johanna's couch, and left the room.

When the children are asleep: Johanna suspected they had told her to stay in bed because they did not want her in the family circle at the funeral, because she was a burden, a bother to the others of whom they were ashamed; nonetheless, no one in the family could take her place, substitute what she had been for Friedrich all these years.

The only people invited to Friedrich's funeral were his siblings, Johanna's daughters and their husbands, whose parents, apart from Lene, were no longer alive. Although Margret intended to send Lene an invitation, it was unlikely that she would leave her village for the funeral service of a distant relative.

Hans came back into the room, arranged a plate and cutlery beside the warming pot, then removed the lid and spooned out peeled boiled potatoes in a dark-brown sauce.

As Johanna was asking him if he could imagine his mother coming to Friedrich's funeral, a potato slipped from the spoon onto the plate and some sauce splattered Johanna's blanket. She grimaced. How did Hans manage to grasp tiny plant parts with his tweezers without damaging them?

Hans apologised and helplessly scanned the room. Johanna told him he would find a cloth in the kitchen. With a red face he lifted the blanket and rubbed vigorously with a dishcloth, making every single brown spot into a larger, light-brown smudge. Johanna rubbed her arms with cold. After a moment she seized the blanket.

As she ate Hans said, "My mother has only once left her village, for my wedding."

Johanna remembered that she and Lene had been introduced for the first time at Hans and Margret's wedding. That was nearly twenty years ago now. All the same, Johanna saw Lene before her, a sturdy woman sitting silently on her chair in a dark-blue knitted dress. Johanna thought for a moment, laid down her fork, asked Hans to open the cupboard and pointed to a rich green album, which he passed to her.

Inside, Johanna found a blurred colour photograph Hans had given to her and Friedrich prior to the wedding. Lene stood in long grey knitted house shoes before a low slate-roof house, her round face framed by a headscarf. Beside her in his buggy sat Erwin. Bare rose bushes lined either side of the path that the couple were standing on, leading to a small bay window from where a barely discernible dark strip indicated the rest of the path. There was no door to be seen – Johanna presumed it was to the right of the photo – and an open window on the left looked little more than a black square, so that Johanna was unable to see inside the house. But behind the closed window of the little conservatory you could make out the shape of pink pot plants and a white curtain.

Johanna looked up and across at Hans, who was hovering next to the wheeled table. Something of the woman was reflected in his face. Unlikely that she could talk to Lene about subjects other than her village.

જી

On the morning of the funeral, Lene, in a calf-length dress that hugged her sturdy figure, came down the stairs to the hall where Margret, Hans and Johanna were waiting. The previous night, Hans had fetched her from the station and brought her to Johanna's house.

Johanna, with one arm leaning on her walking stick, briefly raised her other hand in goodbye. The doctor had recommended she go into the garden three times a day, but insisted she stay away from the funeral because she was intolerant to tranquillisers and without them might collapse again.

The sky had taken on a greyish hue. Standing in the half-open front door, Johanna heard the gentle creak of the garden gate. The others waved back from the street.

Back on the sofa she closed her eyes and sensed Friedrich nearby, a young Friedrich with dark-blonde hair, a fine face, a whole-hearted smile just for her. He was leaning against the glass door of the kitchen sideboard, with crockery and marmalade jars gleaming behind. She was standing across from him at arm's length with her hair worn up.

When she awoke, Johanna thought she was lying in their old attic apartment in Wrocław. In her dazed state she was aware of whispering voices and dark figures creeping through the room, trying to be quiet. She met Tanya's gaze. A few minutes later there was the clatter of crockery as the household help and the other women set the table.

Johanna made an effort to get up and allowed herself to be led to the table. Rosa put Lene in Friedrich's seat. They ate lunch in silence: three couples, two of Rosa's grown-up children, Lene and Johanna. After the meal, as Tanya was leaving, she said, "My children never really knew their Opa."

"Funerals are not for children," responded Margret.

&

Lene's train would not leave until eight o'clock, and so in the afternoon Johanna showed her some of the house. Lene looked around the rooms with scarcely a word, and if she did suddenly comment, Johanna had to listen hard to understand her dialect.

It was quiet now in the house; only the household help hurried across the hallways now and then. Though they hardly exchanged a word, Johanna found Lene's presence not unpleasant; side by side with her, the silence seemed more bearable. She would show Lene her garden. Being a woman from a village, she was bound to like it.

The morning clouds had cleared. Before they went outside, Lene asked for a pair of secateurs and once outside deftly cut a neat armful of dahlias, chrysanthemums and sunflowers, mixing these with late wildflowers.

"You have replaced my gardener," Johanna laughed, as Lene followed her back into the living room and bunched the flowers in a blue vase on the dining table.

"Your garden's no work at all," Lene answered.

After their garden stroll, Johanna lay on the sofa and told Lene to fetch the old armchair from Friedrich's study so that she could sit comfortably – the settee by the door was too hard and narrow – and keep her company a while longer. Effortlessly Lene carried the chair, and as Johanna watched her body glide into it as though it were made for her, dimly she recalled a time when she had set eyes on this chair daily; when, decades ago, it had been part of the living room decor. Now it smelled more strongly of tobacco than the other furniture because it had served Friedrich as his study reading chair.

It occurred to Johanna that Lene was only a few years younger than her and, like her, had lived for over half a century. But she stayed silent, until finally Lene picked up some knitting in red wool and began to knit. Soon the quiet click-clack of the needles had a soothing effect on Johanna.

∞

When Margret came in the early evening to help Johanna wash, as she did every second day, she stumbled over her hello when she saw Lene in Friedrich's old chair; her voice fell to a murmur before eventually ebbing away as she caught sight of the autumn bouquet that partly obscured Lene's upper body.

Johanna had turned on her side so she could see the flowers. As Margret sat down beside her on the sofa, she quietly groaned. Each time she washed she had to climb up and down fifteen wooden stairs polished smooth by the household help. The bathroom was on the top floor, and Johanna had no wish to move there. Friedrich's smell still lingered on the sofa.

With her slender hand, Margret gripped Johanna's upper arm. Johanna buried her head in the pillow, tensed her muscles and held her arm tightly against her body, even though it caused her greater strain. Johanna felt ashamed when she saw Lene put down her knitting, stand up and walk towards her; as she rolled away the table from the bed, Margret let go of her mother's arm in surprise. Lene put a hand under Johanna's shoulder and her other arm around her back. Johanna heard Lene's breathing, sensed her heavy upper body over her. She yielded and relaxed. She felt the strong pressure of Lene's hands through her blouse and cardigan, a pleasant, protective sensation, an energy that transmitted warmth to her body; in contrast, the pressure of Margret's hands was acute, less even, less compact.

Johanna sat up, slowly stood and walked to the foot of the staircase, supported on both sides. Lene guided her hand onto the banister and pressed her fingers firmly around the smooth wood.

Johanna knew Lene was watching as she laboriously climbed up with Margret, stair by stair. They were almost at the top when she turned, straightened her knees and said to Lene, "The top floor is free, because the girls left straight after the funeral. If you wish, stay with me a few more days."

Amazed at what she had said, Johanna went into the bathroom.

∞

Margret led her to the hard stool against the tiled wall, unbuttoned first her cardigan then her blouse and finally unfastened her bra. Johanna shivered from the tiling at her back.

"Did you forget to turn on the heater?" she asked sourly.

Margret turned, silently switched on the heater, waited for the fan noise to even out and continued to undress her – the dark button on her skirt, the worn zip, finally her tights and underwear

– as she had for years; only now, the communal ritual took place more often.

As Johanna stepped into the bath, the inside of her upper thigh brushed the edge. Recently she had felt not only the cold of the enamel but also its hardness. She sat down on the low bath stool. Gradually the room grew warmer.

"Can you imagine, Lene looked after Erwin for twenty years," Margret said, as she vigorously rubbed a facecloth over Johanna's back.

"But I am your mother," Johanna replied truculently.

Margret said nothing, turned on a tap and held the showerhead over the nape of Johanna's neck. Johanna screamed. Margret quickly turned off the tap and apologised, let go of the showerhead and turned away. As she bent over Johanna afresh, she said in a low voice that in her tiredness she had confused the taps.

"You don't know what lack of sleep is!" Johanna retorted angrily. "Which one of us has lost her husband?"

Carefully, Margret turned on one tap, then the other, tested the temperature with her hand and, as she slowly rinsed off the lather from top to bottom, said, "You lost him decades ago."

"No," Johanna responded flatly. "His affair with that woman was a thing of no consequence, after the war."

Margret wrapped Johanna in the bath towel and held her firmly with it. "You misunderstand me," she said gently. "You lost him to his ideas."

"That I have known a long time," Johanna responded, after a pause.

Now, as usual, while Johanna complained about the roughness of the towel, Margret dried her face, neck, belly, back, breasts, upper thighs, bottom and between her legs, helped her over the bath edge and dressed her in silence in fresh clothes: a skirt that looked like the old one and smelled of wash powder, a lighter blouse of the same synthetic material: items of clothing familiar for years.

Afterwards they climbed down the stairs. Margret led Johanna to the dining table and said goodbye with a sideways glance at Lene, who took her seat next to Johanna.

℘

During dinner Lene praised the sausage, the creamy butter, the hearty cheese, and Johanna told her about the things Friedrich had liked to eat, his daily routine, his job at the university. She did not tell her about her morning reverie and her doubt.

"Everyone has to go some time," said Lene in a dry tone.

Johanna gave her a disdainful look. "Yes, but not everyone leaves behind the same."

"Nothing's left, save for the children," replied Lene bluntly.

Johanna shook her head with a frown as she ate.

"I'd like to take you up on your offer," she heard. "So tomorrow will you show me the forest over there?"

Johanna knew without raising her head which forest Lene was referring to; all the same, she followed Lene's extended arm, which was pointing through the glass door to a dark-green hill rising far beyond the garden, dotted with separate patches of orange gold and wine red.

A ridiculous thing to ask, thought Johanna; it cannot have escaped Lene's notice how difficult I find walking.

Johanna shook her head again. "The doctor has forbidden me to walk long distances."

"Doctors haven't a clue," Lene responded. "I'm sure you'll manage."

Johanna sat in stunned silence. Decades ago, Friedrich had once said something similar to her. It had been a winter's day, before the war began, when she had visited him in prison. Under her coat she was carrying Rosa, wrapped in a woollen shawl. At the end of their brief conversation he had said, "I'm quite sure you'll manage."

Johanna dabbed her mouth and hands with her napkin and called the household help. She saw that only now did Lene remove the rolled-up cloth from its silver-plated ring and inelegantly wipe her lips.

Lene stood up, passed Johanna her stick and helped her up. The household help circled round them, stacking plates and glasses on a tray. In a few days Johanna would ask if she wished to eat with her from now on. She could not have tolerated another woman near her and Friedrich.

"Come," she said to Lene. "I'd like to show you something."

Johanna found going up the stairs easier than she had an hour previously. They walked past Lene's room to a wooden door at the end of the hallway, which opened into a low room with sloping ceilings. Through a tiny window a shaft of light fell on the edge of a sofa below. Johanna invited Lene to sit with her and asked her to switch on the dusty standard lamp.

"So that you don't get bored," Johanna said, and with her arm described an arc. "This is *my* library."

"When am I going to read all this, then?" Lene laughed out loud.

"Not all of it at once," Johanna responded.

Lene's eyes roamed the shelves that covered three walls. "There are even cookbooks," she said.

"Now and then I used to like to cook," Johanna replied. On special evenings when Friedrich had visitors, Johanna had carefully chosen a menu with the household help, given her precise instructions and seasoned all the dishes.

"All the recipes I know are from my mother or my grandmother," Lene said.

For a time they gazed at the bookshelves in silence. When eventually Johanna heaved herself up from the couch with a yawn, Lene accompanied her downstairs, handed her her walking stick where the banister ended and made up Johanna's bed on the ground floor.

Before she fell asleep Johanna heard the heavy fall of firm footsteps above her. A door opened and the footsteps faded away in the direction of her library room.

&

Over the following two days, Lene seemed strangely vacant at mealtimes, ate hurriedly and muttered during dessert that she had something to see to upstairs. Again Johanna heard her footsteps, a sound that faded the farther Lene walked from the spare room; then silence reigned until the next meal. Johanna smiled to herself. She did not feel alone, because Lene's presence was tangible in the colourful flower bouquet, the faint smell of sweat that pervaded the house, the sporadic creaking of floorboards above the kitchen, there, where her library was.

Johanna stepped into the garden several times a day and remained there longer than the doctor had advised her to. As she strolled around, her gaze rested longer each time on the autumn hills. At supper on the second day she said to Lene that she would be glad to go on an outing with her.

The following morning, when Johanna and Lene got out at a bus stop not far from the forest, the driver eyed them uncertainly. "There's only forest here," he said.

"I have lived in this city for thirty years," Johanna replied curtly, but did not mention that she had not been to this spot in over ten years.

Here the wind was cooler than in the valley. Without a word, Lene buttoned up her own as well as Johanna's cardigan. Johanna stayed still and surrendered to the kind-hearted gesture. They stood by the bus for a moment to look down on the city. Several hundred metres below the bus stop, allotments began, extending in one direction as far as the terrace-like white apartment blocks. Sunflowers, as well as rose bushes, dahlias and asters planted in rows grew above partly rotten garden cabins. There were rosehip bushes with scrawny branches in front of the fences that enclosed the gardens. In the other direction Johanna saw the little church tower of the village, now merged with the city, where as a young girl Margret had worked for several months.

She tipped back her head and blinked in the sun as it warmed her face. Strange, she thought – in all the time we lived here I never once went for a walk with Friedrich, and until the day before yesterday I hadn't felt the lack.

They came upon a narrow path lined on either side by tall trees, whose tops cast great shadows onto the trail. Johanna walked slowly, supported on her right with her stick and on her left by Lene, but as she walked she did not feel her energy fade; her breathing was deep and even. She could not instantly identify the forest smells, as familiar to her as a childhood friend not seen in several years.

"A landscape like the one in your books," Lene said into the silence.

Johanna turned her head. "There are lots of books that contain nature descriptions," she replied softly, and smiled.

"As children we often gathered mushrooms," Lene continued.

Johanna nodded without answering. She was unsure whether the images that suddenly sprang to mind were from stories she had heard, bits of novels, or her own life. One image lingered longer than the others: at the barracks near Hamburg, after the war, one afternoon Margret had been playing on a sandy bank. The smell of damp, rotten barrack wood hung in the air. Johanna watched Margret play, watched as she dug small hollows in the sand and in each one crushed something earth-coloured to a mushy pulp. Johanna hurried over, beheld the mushroom-covered slope and dragged Margret away, because she did not know the shiny brown fungi. That night Friedrich had told her they were edible, and Johanna had wrapped the remaining ones in an old piece of cloth so that he could cook them in his room.

As if to herself Johanna muttered, "Margret doesn't go for walks with me."

Lene looked over at her.

"She hasn't the time," Johanna added.

"My family was always important to me," Lene said, before quickly adding in a more familiar tone, "At Erwin's funeral she just walked off with the children. I'll never forget that. At the time I thought, I'll show her what it's like when her own father dies, but now I know you, I'm glad I didn't."

In irritation Johanna remembered the morning in the university auditorium and thought that, sometimes, there can be reasons to leave a funeral early.

"Cried, the wee boy did," Lene said. "She didn't have him under control."

When my children were small, Johanna reflected, I had other issues: the children needed food, clothes, an apartment... Lene must have known that, just like me. She hesitated, before addressing Lene more familiarly, "Did you have Hans under control?"

"Of course," Lene replied.

"I don't know," Johanna said thoughtfully, "if I had the girls under control. But all three survived the war."

The forest path led to a clearing. As Johanna saw the leaves glittering in the sun she was gripped by a sensation she knew from evenings with Friedrich's friends. Illness and physical frailty seemed far away. Once more, Johanna felt her heart beat in quite a different rhythm to its familiar palpitations. She stretched herself up tall and wished Friedrich were standing next to her. Then she reverted to her hunched posture. She should have asked him sooner: might he have taken the time to go for a walk with her?

Once more Johanna thought of the evenings she had spent with Friedrich in the circle of academics. It struck her how rarely he had returned her gaze.

"Let's turn round," she said to Lene. "I can't manage any more today."

❧

In the afternoon the doorbell rang. Johanna was resting on the sofa, feeling both refreshed and tired after the morning outing. The household help was busy cleaning the upstairs rooms, so Lene went to the door. Sonja followed her into the living room, placed a plate with a cake on the dining table and leaned diffidently against the table end as Lene sat down in the chair and lowered her head over a book.

Although Sonja appeared gangly and moved awkwardly, her face was open. Johanna could not say whether she looked more like Hans or Margret. She was wearing her thin hair (which Margret always used to cut boyishly short) in a ponytail tied at the back of her head. After a moment, she came to the lower end of the sofa and sat carefully on the edge. She stared at Lene's knitting, a red pullover yet to grow sleeves that could be for her, judging by its width. Sonja's face remained motionless. Suddenly she looked down at her lap, where her hands were clasped.

"Mummy and Daddy were arguing about who should bring the cake. So I brought it."

For a moment Johanna and Lene looked long at each other.

Then Lene muttered, "My Hans helped me a lot."

"Helped how?" asked Sonja.

"D'you remember your Opa?" Lene asked.

Johanna flinched.

"Erwin," added Lene.

Sonja stared through the glass door into the garden. "I still have a doll he made for me," she said.

"He couldn't walk," Lene responded, and heaved herself out of the chair in her own vigorous way. "I'll go put on coffee and milk. And then we'll share the cake."

While a gentle clatter emanated from the kitchen, Sonja drew nearer to Johanna. "Mummy's sick. Yesterday morning she lay in bed, cried and said she didn't want to see anyone. She asked me to call school. Daddy was shouting at her again."

Annoyed, Johanna waved dismissively. "Think of all we've come through."

Sonja stared at her, as though trying to fathom the hidden meaning of her grandmother's words. This look of Sonja did Johanna good, and she wondered whether she should tell the girl about herself. Then Lene pushed open the living room door with her foot.

Not long after that, each of them was eating a piece of the apple cake Margret had baked.

Dancing Daughter

Margret • 1988

'Where are you from, pretty bird?'

'How beautiful you are, with wings the colour of orange, iridescent green tail feathers and a sunshine yellow beak...

'Can't you fly? Show me again your left wing – is it hurt? You can't lift it or spread it. Did someone tear it? Bite it? What do the people want from you, the ones that enclose you in their crude circle? What do they want with their bulky bodies, their rough hands, their greedy eyes? Sharpen your claws, before someone snatches you, strokes your feathers, tenderly yet with ravenous eyes that close in until their hands sink into your feathers to pluck them out...

'You don't care to sing for them anymore? I can understand that, even though I enjoyed hearing you, but do you know that you can also peck with a beak? You wouldn't do such a thing? Watch out for their hands!'

∞

Margret left the hospital on the east side and stood still in the immense brightness of the morning hour. She shut her eyes for a moment in the unfamiliar light as a sweet breeze drifted by. It was a balmy spring day and the sun soothingly warmed her bare forearms. Nevertheless, she felt like a traveller who had just stepped from the train station of some foreign city.

She opened her eyes and tried to find her bearings amidst the nearby buildings, small grassy areas and pavements. She saw small flowers in the grass and people in bright, spring-like clothes, a confusion of colours. Eventually she sat down on the kerbside. As she fought back tears she saw Hans. They had arranged that he would pick her up at the main entrance. The nearer he got the faster he walked, and, when he reached her, without a word he crouched down, took her hand and stroked it. For a while they both remained seated thus, in silence, without looking at one another; and when they got up, Margret's first step wobbled.

At home, Margret wanted to start preparing lunch straight away, but Hans told her she should rest a little longer, and took a packet of soup from the top cupboard. Margret bent down and put a suitable pan on the hob, placed a box of matches beside it and walked reluctantly to the kitchen door. She turned round and saw Hans nod smilingly to her. Softly she shut the door behind her.

In the bedroom she curled up on the bed and hugged her knees. With a shiver of the spine the memory assailed her: she had fallen asleep in the same position and dreamed about a wounded bird that lay helpless on the ground, surrounded by onlookers; the people's faces and hands had threatened her, a danger she did all she could to escape until finally someone with a bright voice, a child perhaps, put the bird in their palm, stroked its feathers and, cupping it safely, quickly carried it away.

Then she had woken up and no sooner realised she was in a hospital than a doctor was waving an empty box of pills at her. Margret recognised the box but could not recall how many pills it had contained, and had simply shrugged.

She sat bolt upright and went back into the kitchen. Soup was simmering on a low flame. She lifted the pot lid. A few pasta shapes were swimming in a thin, salty-smelling stock. Margret was relieved it neither looked nor smelled like Lene's noodle soup.

Hans was standing at the living room window and turned round when she came over. "Lie a little longer," he insisted.

"Who found me?" Margret asked, taking a deep breath and holding it in.

Hans looked apprehensive, avoiding her gaze.

"You?" she said, exhaling.

Hans shook his head. "Sonja called the ambulance." He added, murmuring, "I've tried to talk to her."

Margret nodded, lost in thought. Sonja, unlike Hans and Sebastian, had not visited her in hospital. However, Margret hadn't thought it strange; lately, Sonja had spent limited time with them and was often out with friends instead, without saying where they went. In the evenings she asked Sonja to phone home if she would be late, but she never did, not even when she returned after midnight. Sometimes her clothes smelled of cigarette smoke, and Margret wondered whether she should simply take her daughter's clothes out of her room and put them in the washing machine; but she let it be.

At breakfast, Sonja often seemed scarcely able to stay awake, and would remain silent when Margret said a few inconsequential words to her. This silence rendered Margret helpless. A few weeks previously, the teacher had demanded a written apology for Sonja's daylong absence from class, and Margret had handed in the letter without discussing it with Sonja, even though she had known nothing of her absence. Over this period Sonja had left the apartment in the morning and returned in the afternoon, and her school marks had not suffered.

Margret bit her lip, pressed her teeth into the flesh. Six months ago her mother had died; Margret had not needed to shake her to know she was dead. In the last weeks Margret had spent every night with her, in the old living room armchair which she pushed into her parents' bedroom. While her mother slept in the double bed, Margret listened to her gentle snoring, and the instant it stopped, anxiously held her breath for several seconds, then got up and went over to her. In the darkness she bowed her head over her mother and confirmed her weak breathing. Once, she caressed her cheek – it was night and she hoped her mother would not push her away – and got goose bumps on touching her mother's thin skin, which looked pallid by day. Her mother had not fought her off, but instead murmured Margret's father's name with a smile.

Her mother no longer spoke during the day, but some nights she would talk for hours. She mumbled and her words made no sense, but Margret listened to her, strangely moved.

Then, one night – her mother had fallen asleep in the early evening as usual – a definitive silence set in. For a time Margret sat mutely on the bed before beginning the funeral arrangements and the dissolution of the household.

What must Sonja have felt when she had been unable to waken her?

Only gradually did Margret's thoughts return to the present. She heard Hans say, "She shouted at me," and when she realised whom he meant, she wondered how it was possible he had tried to talk with Sonja.

∞

The doctor gave Margret sick leave until the summer holidays. She went regularly to a psychologist, whom she told about some difficult pupils and her father's books, and who told her after her third session that she would have no problem returning to work in the coming school year.

On other days she got up before the children, prepared their breakfast and then caught up with the housework that had been neglected over recent weeks. She took down the curtains and washed them, dusted all the wardrobes, defrosted the freezer, tidied the clothes in the wardrobes, sorted through her blouses and skirts, threw out obsolete teaching materials and tidied her desk drawers. The day she hung up the curtains again, down on the army barracks one of the soldiers, a young slim man, raised his hand uncertainly, and Margret raised hers in surprise.

The following afternoon Margret phoned a male colleague she had been friendly with for a long time and invited him round for the three free hours he had every other week. Martin was no more than ten years older than her and, like her, had two children and lived with his family in one of the blocks in the north of the city. Many pupils liked him because in language lessons they would listen to English and American songs, some of which were not played on East German radio stations: rock ballads, political songs, love songs. Martin told Margret that he endeavoured to give the pupils time after listening to gradually reemerge from the music, that he would always start by asking if they had liked the song, and why; and he told her that some pupils, who otherwise hardly spoke, suddenly knew how to express themselves surprisingly well in English. He also thought he had seen how the young people within a class would then treat each other more mindfully.

Martin had short grey hair and no moustache. He greeted Margret warmly but without being overly familiar; he clasped her hand in his, gently inclined his head towards her and looked her in the eye.

Once they had sat down, coffee cups before them on the table, he asked delicately, "You didn't want to die, but sleep, isn't that right?"

As he studied her face, Margret blushed and tried to hide her confusion. She had long stopped asking herself what she had wanted, and found it even stranger that another person should ask. She nodded, because she was unable to string together the words in her head. She thought the ring of the tram outside sounded shrill, after not having noticed it in years.

"And what do you want now, right this moment?" Martin asked in a clear, calm voice. He filled the chair on which he sat upright, as though in no doubt that he was at the right place here and now, as though he had never asked himself if his presence were desired, as though his existence were simply taken for granted.

Talk with you, then cook dinner, wait for the children, Margret had wanted to reply, but Martin stood up and walked to the window; automatically, her eyes followed him. From the table she could not see the barracks but instead a lush green beyond low grey houses, a shimmering blue sky, dazzling light that cast Martin's long shadow onto the carpet.

"I would like," Margret said with care, as though she first had to test the sound and sense of her words, "to go away for a few days."

"Where to?"

"Lake Balaton, the Black Sea, Prague..." Margret said.

"How about Greece, Finland, Canada?"

"We are teachers," she replied.

"When you pursue the impossible, you will achieve incredible things."

She knew he was wrong. A few weeks previously, Margret had visited her pupils unannounced in the factory they worked in twice a month. Production work was part of their curriculum, accompanied by a theoretical part called "Introduction to Socialist Production", comprising theoretical and practical classes held over alternate weeks.

Margret was assaulted by the noise of the machinery in the windowless, artificially lit production hall that reeked of oil, sweat, metal and urine. The toilets were on the left-hand side, next to the hall entrance. The floor manager was nowhere to be seen, so Margret went past several lathes to a separate alcove. Here some workers were seated in a circle eating breakfast and talking animatedly, but they fell silent when Margret addressed them. They were clutching liverwurst or salami sandwiches in hastily washed hands that still bore traces of oily dirt, and even above the machinery din Margret could hear their loud masticating and swallowing. They eyed Margret half-dismissively, half-suggestively, until one of them got up, brushed the greasy crumbs from his fingers and put a hand on her shoulder. She was wearing a light-blue dress and was at a loss as to how to shake off his hand without causing offence. But the man removed it himself and pointed in the direction of a barely discernible door at the end of the hall. "Down there, lady – that's the way to the floor manager."

As she quietly thanked him, she heard another, younger man whisper, "I bet she gets double what I get – at least a thousand."

Margret hurriedly turned to go.

The floor manager was wearing the same ink-blue bib overalls as the other workers. They met in front of the office from which he had just emerged, and he held open the door into the dark room for her. When she told him she wanted to visit her pupils, he closed the door and locked it from outside.

As they shook hands she noticed that his were warm and clean. It was only now, as they walked down the middle of the hall between the machinery, that Margret noticed the colours of the place: olive-green and black, the dull silver of steel. They waded through metal shavings, the sound of their footsteps on the stone floor was drowned out by the machinery, the light glared down coldly from above; there was a danger that human beings were ignored, Margret reflected. Suddenly two of her pupils appeared behind a lathe: two thin boys, one of whom was working at the lathe while the other watched on. Beside them, the lathe operator was supervising. When he saw Margret he said to her, "I told him he's to explain it to his pal."

Margret saw how the "pal", a weedy pupil with a squint, did his best to follow the procedure and memorise the sequence. Drops of spittle shone on his tightly pressed lips.

After the turning was finished and the supervisor had approved the small metal part and offered the pupil some scant praise for his work, Margret greeted both boys. Then the "pal" took over from the other boy, stepped – cheeks now red – behind the lathe and inserted a fresh piece of metal. After a furtive glance at Margret he started the machine, but because she was standing on the other side, she was unable to see what his hands were doing and only noticed how his head glowed and his skinny arms became more frenzied. Then he cursed several times under his breath and switched off the machine. The supervisor extracted the part from inside. It appeared to have slipped off-centre. It lay mangled in his palm, and he whistled derisively between his teeth and lower lip. Finally, he offhandedly slipped the useless part into the reject box. The other pupil broke into laughter, guffawing and gloating as though he now felt a release of tension.

That same afternoon, Margret had spoken up at the party meeting and described what she had witnessed at the factory. It was not the first time she had outlined to the other teachers how she viewed her pupils. She was too pessimistic, they usually said, preferring to see her pupils' bad side; she underestimated their capacity to develop. This time her colleagues were silent; only the party secretary said, with a condescending smile and a look that blatantly cast doubt on Margret's observational powers, that she must be exaggerating somewhat.

Later she left the meeting without a word.

∞

Martin was leaning with his back to the window, arms folded, facing Margret. She appreciated the fact that he neither quizzed her nor explained to her where her problems lay. She would have liked to tell him more about herself, but the words seemed to stick in her throat.

With a jerk Martin lifted his slender body from the sill and went over to the central section of a wall unit where, behind two small glass doors, various photographs and fine ceramic objects were displayed.

"Is that your mother?"

Margret nodded.

"Have you more photos?"

Hesitantly she stood up, went into the next room and returned with a bundle of black-and-white photographs, which she handed to Martin. In her hands she felt the firmness of the top photo and the thin paper of the bottom one. Martin spread out the photos on the dinner table so that they formed a line: there was her mother next to Sebastian, Sebastian next to her father, her father beside Hans, Hans beside her big sister, Rosa beside Sonja. Margret stared down at them. All were smiling, and no picture corresponded with the person photographed; these all showed a particular pose, a facial expression deliberately adopted at a moment in life, or else captured by the photographer.

"And where would you put your photo?" Martin asked.

Spontaneously Margret slid apart Sonja's and Rosa's pictures and pointed to the gap. Then she studied the entire line again, beginning with Sonja and ending with her mother, whose portrait Margret gazed at longer than the others: her soft cheeks, her hazelnut-brown hair, a strand sitting on her forehead. Again she saw her mother on her deathbed, her body growing inexorably thinner, her skeletal limbs, the garden beyond, a branch softly swaying at the window, and finally she saw herself as she calmly notified the doctor of her death.

She began to choke, feared she would vomit, but brought up only words as she sobbed and, staring at her handkerchief, rambled on incoherently about Rosa, who had completely cut her off, and had, like

Tanya, refused to help with their mother; about her mother and about Sonja; about the other people in the photographs. And only when she had stopped talking, with no idea of how much time had passed, did she notice the soaked ball in her hands. She was embarrassed to put it on the table so went into the other room and dropped it in the laundry basket.

Back in the living room, Margret apologised and sat on a chair. Martin shook his head, stepped behind her, laid both hands on her shoulders and briefly pressed. Margret could have shaken off his hands; she could have laid a hand over his, or stood up, but instead she let her head sink back with her eyes shut and gave a start when her hair brushed the fabric of his shirt. All the same, she stayed sitting thus, and felt his stomach support her head.

When Martin gave her shoulders another press and said he would come to see her again soon, she opened her eyes.

She accompanied him into the hall, where he briefly brushed her forearm, turned and left. Margret shut the door. Then she sat down again at the dinner table and stared at his cup, which still contained more than half the coffee she had poured for him.

∞

That night, for the first time Sonja was still not home by two in the morning. Margret woke up the mother of one of her friends with an anxious phone call and learned there was a party at the *Junge Gemeinde*†. Unlike her friend, Sonja had never mentioned that she attended *Junge Gemeinde* meetings and, even though Margret now knew where Sonja was, she remained worried.

In her dressing gown, she sat at the living-room table under the standard lamp, its harsh light illuminating the wall unit, television, couch, as well as her pictures that had hung on the walls for years: a Madonna and Child; an icon picture; a painting from Nicaragua depicting a village with brightly dressed children running, a sky-blue river, adobe huts, a straw-yellow field in the distance. Margret found the pictures strangely reassuring, as was Sebastian's soft snoring next door.

Last year they had reorganised their apartment so that Sebastian and Sonja could each have their own room. Now the children's room was her and Hans's bedroom, and also housed Margret's desk; meanwhile, Sebastian had festooned her old study walls with fringed football pennants. Margret hardly ever worried about Sebastian; he rarely went out, and then only on Saturdays, when he cheered on his favourite team at the stadium and then recounted it over supper, jubilant and enthused or disappointed, the same way he spoke about his classmates and teachers.

She padded across the hall to Sonja's room, their old bedroom, and turned on the light. The wall above Sonja's bed was plastered with poems, song lyrics and photos cut out of newspapers. One photo showed two boys with contrasting skin and hair, a white dove with wings outspread perched on the hands of the dark-skinned boy; another picture showed the two lovers by Chagall next to an oversized daisy bouquet, dancing across a yellow wooden floor as a bright red bird flew around them. Margret read some of the handwritten lines and rediscovered a well-known poem, "Two Rowing a Boat"* – so apparently Sonja also longed for someone, someone who would dare the long voyage at sea with her and stay the course. Sonja was sixteen, Margret forty-four. What colour, what aspect would Margret and Hans's sea have in their memory? Deep turquoise, foaming with turbulent swell, briny, polluted, cold…?

It was the first time Margret had studied Sonja's wall, and suddenly she understood that her daughter dreamed of nothing other than what Margret had longed for once: an unconditional love and a fairer world; and yet, for Sonja, these wishes had other colours and forms to those they had had for Margret.

She turned off the light again and lay in bed beside Hans. Did he know the unconquerable fear that kept her awake? She turned to look at him. A thin shaft of moonlight shone past the curtains and illuminated his cheeks, his forehead, his closed eyes. On his chin, scarcely visible black stubble stood out from his pale skin. Early tomorrow he would shave it off. The lines that ran from temple to temple had grown more numerous; his skin looked rough. Margret felt her own face and noted its rough texture. How soft, on the other hand, Sonja's and Sebastian's faces had been when last she had caressed them. It must be months ago now.

Outside, it was gradually getting light. Margret felt an aching urgency to touch her children's skin. After a while she heard the click of a key and listened to the noises in the apartment until Sonja had changed in the bathroom and shut her door behind her.

∞

The following afternoon Margret listened at Sonja's door. Songs accompanied by guitar chords emanated from within. Sonja's voice rang gently. Margret knocked. When she entered, Sonja blushed and laid the guitar on her carelessly made bed. Suddenly Margret realised how small and restrictive the room was as she reached the window in three or four paces along a narrow aisle cluttered with furniture on either side. She looked down at the view. A few people were waiting for the tram, and across the tracks the Soviet soldiers were drilling. Perhaps in the evening one of them would take out his accordion.

"Was the party nice?" Margret turned to Sonja, trying her best to sound casual.

The colour drained from Sonja's face, and she froze. But she mumbled a yes, and Margret felt herself perspire, relieved at Sonja's concession but keen to say nothing wrong.

"And so what did you do?"

"Just what you do at parties – sang, danced, chatted."

"D'you go there often?"

Sonja was silent for a moment, before blurting out, "You haven't a clue! At least the minister's doing something, so that something changes round here!"

Margret thought she understood, but replied that it was time to think about her leaving exams. Impassively Sonja raised then lowered her shoulders, before adding with a childlike glint in her eyes, "Why don't you come with me some time?"

They were standing opposite each other, and Margret sensed the space between them like a chasm that would only deepen if she turned down Sonja's seemingly casual invitation. She glanced at Sonja's wall. Nothing is unalterable, she said to herself to fight her fears, as long as neither she nor Sonja remained like stone.

She still owed Sonja an answer when she left her room.

৪৩

On the main street, a nondescript door led through a short passageway into a courtyard. "Christians and Marxists need one another" was written in thick bright marker on a strip of white sheet hanging above the entrance to an unstable-looking side wing. The plasterwork here, unlike that to the front, was crumbling away. On a remaining piece, Margret caught the flash of a dove with outspread wings painted in white. She thought of the photograph on Sonja's wall. In the yard were bicycles with chipped paint and buckled wheels, various buckets with dried paint dripped over the edges, old drinks crates, a table tennis table, and to the left a wooden table with benches in front of a few unkempt bushes.

Inside the building an arrow on a piece of card pointed up narrow stairs. When Margret entered the only first-floor room with the door open, the people already there turned towards her. They were predominantly young people of Sonja's age dressed in loose T-shirts, thin jeans or other cotton trousers; nothing out of the ordinary, clothes suitable for the balmy spring night, perhaps with a little more vibrancy and colour than most pupils' everyday attire. Margret recognised a boy and girl she taught and reddened under their surprised stares.

They had agreed to go separately. That morning, when Margret hastily outlined Sonja's invitation to Hans, he had jumped up, aghast.

"What's she seeking in a religious institution? Wouldn't it be better to take her away from there?" he had asked.

"What do you think it's like at one of these meetings?" Margret had inquired.

"Don't know," he had replied.

Margret sat in one of the farthest rows of hastily arranged chairs and looked around a room half the size of a classroom, adorned with Bible quotes, each one occupying an entire wall. In the middle of the room was a step, so that from the front it looked like a low stage. On a piano to the side lay some songbooks.

From the courtyard came the bright, happy sound of girls' voices, then Margret heard stamping on the stairs. She turned to the door, which had a sign to the left fixed with drawing pins: "Please smoke outside in the yard". When Sonja entered with two other girls she was giggling like a child, as Margret had not seen her do in a long time. Sonja gave her a quick wave and pushed past several chairs with her friends to sit at the end of the first row.

Eventually the minister appeared, a plump, roughly forty-year-old man with long, carelessly combed hair tied in a ponytail, dressed in faded jeans and a green cotton shirt. Once he had sat on the stage, the young people talked more quietly or broke off their conversations. Margret's two pupils looked at him expectantly. She felt envious when she saw how much attention they both bestowed him.

Before the minister began, he got up from the stage with surprising verve and took two strides forwards. He reminded them of their last afternoon together, when he had suggested they invite friends and family along tonight, regardless of their Weltanschauung; he was glad to see that some had taken him up on his offer and hoped they would get to speak with each other.

He chose his words with care, as he did when he moved on to describe the long-standing friendships between Christians and Marxists and their common tradition in the antifascist resistance struggle. Then he outlined a framework for a utopian society whereby he connected Marx's prediction of a life without exploitation with the biblical call to be of help to one another. To finish, he asked why they were so far from this ideal, and what they could do to bring themselves closer to it without marginalising anyone in the process.

One of Sonja's friends came forward and said angrily that she didn't understand why at school they talked constantly about Marx but never about the church.

"Marx this, Honecker that, you get sick of it," she exclaimed.

A stocky boy next to her nodded and muttered, "And if you don't say Marx is the greatest, straight away you get a five."

Another boy challenged this by saying, "You're just too scared to speak your mind."

Margret followed the things the young people said (insofar as she could make out individual voices in the babble) with the same eagerness as the minister, who was leaning with his elbows on the piano, apparently with no intention of intervening.

Suddenly she caught sight of Sonja and heard her surprisingly firm-sounding voice, "In my opinion the school should be overhauled. Some of the teachers are simply incompetent."

For a moment it was quiet. Then a few girls giggled furtively, amongst them Margret's pupil. Margret lowered her head: yes, Sonja was right, whether or not she included her mother in that judgement. Just then Margret would have liked to feel Martin's hand on her shoulder, and she thought of the photos. This time she slid Sonja's and her father's photos to the front, and as she did so, Sonja's photo gradually merged into a photo that showed Margret as a roughly twenty-year-old woman in a lecture theatre as she attacked and provoked her father. All of a sudden Margret was certain that Sonja had not been referring to her own suitability for the teaching profession, and that her daughter's often abrasive manner, her seeming inapproachability, masked her fear of trusting anyone – her fear that her trust could be abused.

Now Sonja was having a lively discussion with the other youngsters, who each spoke in turn, with the minister occasionally intervening to urge respect for the person talking. When Sonja suggested they compile a wall newspaper in her school about this evening's theme and asked who thought it a good idea, almost all the young people raised their arms. Surprised at herself, Margret had no hesitation in voicing her own approval too.

After the minister had brought the meeting to an end, Sonja discussed with him which materials they could use. Gradually the others left the room. The minister noted several book titles on a crumpled piece of paper. Sonja did not look up when Margret went downstairs.

In the courtyard Margret hovered uncertainly near the door, slightly away from the youngsters. In the dusk the yard looked unreal and makeshift, like a place of refuge for people who could no longer take their quiet ordered life in their apartments, in front of their televisions. Margret gazed up at the roofs of the surrounding buildings, which looked as unstable as the plasterwork on the meeting house.

After a while Sonja came bounding down the stairs, brushed past Margret with the words, "Bye, see you later!" and joined a small group. She took the cigarette a boy offered her.

&

A few days later, Martin came to visit in the early afternoon. He brought Margret a bouquet of narcissi. Again they sat at the living room table to have coffee, and Martin told her about school. After a time, he leaned over and whispered, "The head's heard about your evening at the *Junge Gemeinde*; there's been talk about you in the staffroom."

"The *Junge Gemeinde*'s a place for exchange," Margret said.

"Yes," Martin nodded. "All the same, you should be a bit more careful."

"It's only the children I fear for," Margret replied.

A silence fell. Martin seemed deep in thought. Then he asked, "Not for you and your husband?"

Margret looked at him with her chin cupped in her hand, and slowly shook her head.

Martin kept his voice down as he told her that for years now his wife had become unapproachable, inexplicably distant from him, and that he was at a loss as to how or when it had started. It was the first time Martin had spoken about his wife; for Margret it presented a suitable opportunity to finally talk at length about the misunderstandings and hostilities between herself and Hans, the hitting and the cold nights. But she was unable to. She took it as given that, because Hans had no friends, he would never talk about her like Martin had about his wife; the idea that her husband would sit with another woman in some living room or café and moan about Margret was so distasteful to her that, when Martin seemingly casually laid his hand on hers, after brief hesitation she withdrew it, even though she would have liked to surrender to the moment, to the affectionate gesture, to the slight arousal she felt. She saw astonishment in Martin's eyes; no disappointment or discouragement. He put his arms around her across the table and the coffee cups. And as she felt the touch of his warm fingers on her nape, his warm, rough cheeks on hers, the little kisses on her neck, her gaze fell on the narcissi, whose buds had straightened slightly and opened.

She pulled away, and Martin sank back into his chair, breathless and bewildered.

∞

In the reception outside the headmaster's office, the secretary was tapping industriously at her typewriter. The rapid click of the lever heads filled the room, interrupted only by a periodic whizz when she completed a line and pressed the carriage lever. Now and then she gave Margret a look over her glasses, partly sympathetic, partly stern.

Margret had been waiting for over an hour and her hands were clammy. She stared numbly at the opaque curtains, whose lace borders brushed fleshy leaves that drooped down like so many tongues, the dark-green leaves of similar-looking, flowerless plants in white pots standing in a row on the windowsill.

Eventually the office door opened and the headmaster came towards her. As ever, his silvery white hair was elegantly combed into a light quiff. He was a tall man, and when he walked along the corridor the pupils made way for him on either side. Margret stood up, discreetly wiped her hands on her skirt and gave him her hand.

"Comrade Gräf," he greeted her with a thin, severe smile, and showed her into his room.

Standing stiffly beside the black faux-leather armchair he offered her were the school's party secretary and gym teacher.

Margret sank into the armchair and reached for the armrests, feeling the three men's gazes on her hair. The faux leather stuck coolly to her hands. Once the headmaster had sat down on a tall chair behind his desk, the other two relaxed, and each leaned a leisurely elbow on Margret's chair back.

"You have always been one of our most reliable comrades," the headmaster said, waving his arm in the air. "And naturally, you are still, is that not correct?"

Margret watched his performance and made no reply.

The party secretary laid his hand familiarly on Margret's shoulder, and she shook it off with a jerk. Then he walked in front of the desk (without obstructing her view of the headmaster) and looked her in the face as you might a child you were half-seriously disciplining for her stupidity.

"Please would you tell me why you have invited me to this interview?" Margret asked the headmaster.

Not a strand stirred of his carefully combed hair as he stood, pressed his hands onto his desk, bent his upper body far over and whispered, "Do you think, dear Comrade Gräf, that your father, who was an upstanding communist, would have approved of his daughter and granddaughter smoking the opium of the people?"

"The meeting was about Christians and Marxists working together," she answered curtly, as if he had only been speaking about her.

Suddenly she asked herself why the gym teacher, who hardly ever spoke and only ever reluctantly, was also present.

"As far as I know, you have two children," the headmaster continued, "and your son appears to be a good child." He broke off, walked to the window, lifted a curtain end and looked outside. "But if you or your daughter continue to associate with these circles, it could conceivably have grave effects on your children's careers; aside from which, we need to ask ourselves whether you are still fit to assume responsibility over your pupils." The white curtain end fell, and Margret met the headmaster's icy stare.

Instinctively she pulled herself up from the armchair, but at the same instant felt the gym teacher's firm hand as he determinedly pushed her back down.

"Do not be impolite," the headmaster said, with the corners of his mouth barely raised: a smile similar to the one he had greeted her with. Then, as the gym teacher took a surprisingly smart step back, the headmaster walked to the armchair and gave Margret his hand. "Goodbye, Comrade Gräf."

As Margret stood up, towards the other side, a smacking noise echoed in the room as she left the seat. She shook hands with each of the three men and walked as calmly and erect as possible through the door the headmaster held open. In the reception hall, out of the corner of her eye she saw the secretary smirking, and behind her the tongue-like plant leaves. Margret felt sick.

❧

At home Margret searched frantically for Sonja's timetable, which she had copied out of her homework jotter at the start of term. At around half-past twelve she left the house and waited by the entrance steps to Sonja's school. When she saw her in a group of schoolgirls, Margret waved and walked quickly towards her daughter, who reluctantly bade goodbye to the others. While Margret told her what had happened that morning, Sonja stared at the pavement.

"Blackmailers," she hissed, and clenched her fists. "They want to intimidate us."

"But you won't go there again," Margret said.

"Yes I will," Sonja replied. "There's nothing wrong in it."

Margret began to panic, talked in a tirade about the threat to Sonja's leaving exams, her future studies, Sebastian; but because Sonja stayed silent, she adopted an increasingly imploring tone. Finally, she gave up and was likewise silent. She thought again of the headmaster, then suddenly of her father as a young man in a tiny room with stone walls, surrounded by savagely smiling, uniformed men. He had never told her the details of his time in prison. Seamlessly Margaret saw him in his departmental office standing behind his desk, dressed in a suit and bow tie, with hair as elegant as the headmaster's, and opposite him on a wooden chair a student, towards whose face her father leaned as the headmaster had towards hers; only there had been few faux-leather armchairs in those days, and men wore not patterned ties but plain dark ones, not light poplin jackets but jackets made of heavy, dark material. But what was deemed right and wrong was already established. And for that reason the student looked afraid, his eyelids flickered, he scratched his hands; for that reason his knees knocked involuntarily and he bit his lower lip until it hurt.

And yet her father was not like the headmaster. He lacked the coldness in the eyes, and he had never blackmailed someone with their family; instead, he might have banged his fists on the desk, threatened to make the student give a public account of himself, claimed he would be expelled from the Party, deregistered, and perhaps said in an overly loud voice, "What you think, young man, is wrong – it flouts the historical laws!"

But her father would not have put on such a performance. Quickly Margret cast aside the thought that she could be deceiving herself. She stopped, took Sonja's wrist and looked pleadingly into her eyes.

Sonja shook her head and repeated, "There's nothing wrong in it."

&

One afternoon in May, Sonja slid her opened homework jotter across the living room table to Margret, who read: "Sonja is receiving a warning because she has displayed a public wall newspaper against the will of the school board. Should there be any further incident she will be precluded from leaving exams and required to repeat tenth grade."

Margret signed Sonja's jotter and passed it back. As Sonja briskly put it in with her books, on the inside of her leather satchel Margret spotted, along with her daughter's name, those of singer-songwriters and rock musicians whose names she had gone over repeatedly. Written across the flap in block capitals was *Gorbi*†; instead of dotting the "i", Sonja had drawn a small star in red pen.

Sonja shouldered her satchel and plodded out of the room. In the doorway she turned again and said in a quiet voice, "Don't worry, I'll manage."

She made it sound as though she had to look after her mother, as though Margret were a frightened child and Sonja her mother.

When in June the exam period began, Margret was relieved. Sonja seemed to sail through her written exams. Whenever Margret asked how she had done, Sonja waved it aside with a smile. On the eve of her first oral exam, Margret ironed Sonja's *FDJ* blouse and her plain dark-blue skirt. As she was about to go to bed, an aroma of coffee filled the apartment. It was almost midnight and Sonja was leaning on the kitchen counter, eyes half-closed, blowing reverently on the surface of her freshly made coffee. When Margret advised her to go to bed, Sonja said, "I'm not quite done yet."

Margret walked past to the open window and looked out into the clear, balmy summer night and wished she were outside, on a beach, in the forest or in a courtyard draped with garlands. She pictured the scene as musicians played, and their violin and flute melodies floated into the high night sky along with the laughter of partygoers, holding each other as they danced thirstily, their faces glowing red. They would be wearing loose, light, colourful clothing.

She shut the window and turned towards Sonja, who like her was gazing into the distance. With head lowered she took a step towards her daughter. She remembered the profundity of the chasm. Sonja did not recoil. As Margret walked past, she gently brushed Sonja's cheek and wished her good night.

The following morning, after waving Sonja goodbye – Sonja waved back for an unusually long time – Margret took the tram to the travel agent's.

When she got back she hurried up the stairs, and as soon as she opened the door she heard quiet sobbing. She went into the living room. Sonja was sitting at the dinner table, wiping her face with the damp sleeves of her *FDJ* blouse.

Truculently she said, "The stupid goat gave me a four."

Margret knew Sonja did not like her English teacher, who was also the school's deputy head; and though she hardly knew her and until now had only met her a few times, she understood why. She remembered something Martin had said (he had occasionally met this teacher at further training events): "One of those who sucks the blood of others, if there is someone she can sell it to." And she remembered that, of course, the headmasters of Sonja's school and the one she taught at were friends.

Margret reached for Sonja's hand and asked her to tell her about the exam.

"It started off quite well," Sonja said. "There wasn't much wrong with my text translation. But I wasn't sufficiently prepared for the next questions and started to stutter. Then, when I saw her gloating smile, I couldn't string a sentence together."

Sonja's blood for her school headmaster, thought Margret angrily: instead of money, the English teacher would be assured of her lifelong right to the office of deputy head; whereby she would never challenge the head for his post either.

Margret took Sonja in her arms and pressed her head against her breast, where she felt spreading an unfamiliar, exhilarating warmth. Sonja's hair was soft and fine and smelled different now to how it had in her childhood. Nevertheless, Margret felt as though she were with an overgrown infant.

After a while Sonja freed herself, looked at Margret from her puffed face and whispered, "And while we were standing alone in the corridor after the exam, she said to me, 'I should really have given you a five. Your grandfather would be ashamed of you.'"

Despite her dismay, Margret calmly shook her head and told Sonja she had a surprise for her. She pointed to two tickets at the edge of the table.

※

When they arrived in Prague, Margret and Sonja hurried directly to Charles Bridge. Leaning against the balustrade they watched the river's languid flow; then Margret straightened, lifted her gaze and looked around her. The stone sculptures lining the balustrade looked huge, the people in the distance tiny. The sun shone down on the city, on the domes and church spires, the red roofs and the sweeping crowns of trees lining the riverbanks, in some places their shade darkening the water's surface.

"Beautiful," Sonja said softly, and Margret thought the same. Again she leaned with her arms on the cold wall.

"What did Dad actually say about us coming to Prague?" Sonja asked, glancing sidelong at her.

"Not much," Margret replied. "That you'd earned it, despite the one failed exam." She paused. "And he said I should persuade you to stop going to *Junge Gemeinde* next term."

"Why?"

"Perhaps he also fears for you."

Sonja gave her a dubious, slightly contemptuous look.

"He must've thought over some things," Margret said.

"I cannot understand," said Sonja, "why you haven't left him."

Margret was silent. She thought of the countless moments when she would have liked to leave and how the everyday, the household, the children, her own weakness had held her back. Hans no longer hit her; instead, he looked out for her, cooked, shopped, even washed the clothes.

"At first, when I saw you lying like that," Sonja said almost inaudibly, "I thought he'd given you the pills."

"He would not have done that," replied Margret, horrified.

A guitar struck up behind them; Sonja turned, trying to spot the musician through the few gaps in the stream of people.

"Come on," she said, and wriggled her way through the crowds to a young bearded man playing the instrument perched on the opposite balustrade. Margret followed and sat a little apart from them both.

"We're spreading the gospel," the young man said, carefully laying his guitar against the balustrade and fixing his gaze on Sonja.

Margret knew he would underestimate Sonja, and chuckled to herself as she began to quiz him and argue heatedly. As they talked, Margret watched the people stroll by and caught only the occasional word of their discussion: human, socialism, church, Big Bang. When the man jumped down from the balustrade, opened his black guitar case, took out a leaflet and handed it to Sonja, her daughter raised her hands in refusal and breezily said goodbye.

Margret slipped off the wall and waited as Sonja came up to her and grunted with a shake of her head. "He says we should accept the world as God created it."

They sauntered towards the end of the bridge with the archway and the two towers of differing height. As they passed underneath, their footsteps echoed on the uneven surface. Several hundred metres ahead to their right rose Prague Castle, mighty, extensive, the pointed towers of the cathedral in the middle.

It was now midday. The city was full of tourists. Margret and Sonja turned down a quieter lane; Margret leaned with her back to the wall and felt the coolness of the stone through the thin fabric of her dress. She drew her index finger over the reddish stonework, felt the bumps and the hollows, the wall's profile, and it felt as though she were rubbing over chalk: an odd, resistant smoothness.

The house facades were painted in warm matte tones. From the window arches, mythical creatures of stone with the heads of women and men looked down at her. Perhaps they could tell her something about the houses and their former inhabitants; Margret would have liked to listen to their stories. Only now did she realise how little she knew about Prague. Neither in Sonja's nor Sebastian's history books had she ever read anything about the history of this city, which struck a chord within her that she had not heard in years, and the resulting ring resonated throughout her being and made her restless.

"Where'll we go?" she asked.

"Up to the castle, I thought," Sonja replied.

"No, we'll go and sit in a café, and tonight we'll go dancing. The castle will still be there tomorrow, and we'll need a good view of the city before we leave."

Sonja made no reply. While Margret kept an eye out for a suitable café she sensed, as so often, Sonja's scrutinising gaze.

∞

At dusk, when the air had cooled, the people emerged from their houses again: local families, youngsters with cassette recorders blaring music, groups of children playing, couples young and old. Margret took in their different skin colours, voices and languages, the sound of their footsteps echoing on the cobblestones, the smells of sweat, perfume and spices.

Hunting for a suitable dance venue, Sonja stared after a group of young girls with brownish complexions, wearing multicoloured flowing skirts like her. A dark-haired girl waved with a laugh, and Sonja waved back.

At the next corner, Margret turned at the sound of someone running up the lane behind them. On reaching them the dark-haired girl caught her breath, then took Sonja's arm familiarly, smiled and, indicating down the lane, asked in English, "D'you want to come with me and my girlfriends?"

Sonja gave Margret an inquiring look and stammered (likewise in English), "We're looking for somewhere to go dancing."

The girl nodded, looking to Sonja then to Margret, still with her friendly smile. Eventually the three of them walked back in the direction from which Margret and Sonja had come, and at the bottom of the lane turned onto a side street. Soon after, they heard a whirlwind drum solo that faded into loud applause. The small, grilled windows the music emanated from were almost at street level.

Sonja and the girl pulled open the solid door, their hands one on top of the other on the metal handle, their bare, summery shoulders colliding, and they glided down a flight of stone steps to a cellar vault into a narrow corridor so full of people that Margret feared losing sight of Sonja in the throng. Instinctively she reached for her hand. Sonja withdrew it and shouted that they would meet later at the exit. Margret stretched and saw through a gap between heads, shoulders, necks, backs and stomachs that Sonja and the dark-haired girl had gone to sit with the girl's friends at one of the oblong tables. The other girls shuffled up to make room for them.

Lightheaded and disarmed by the cigarette smoke and beery haze, Margret made her way deeper into the room, between tables laid out in close lines. Before she saw the band, she heard the singer's foreign voice amplified by the microphone. Then the guitarist started up, and the drummer set the beat for everyone to follow. Margret too swayed and hummed along to the song without understanding the lyrics. In no time the small, round dance floor filled. Margret spotted Sonja amongst the dancers, her head moving to the music, her eyes shut, arms waving nimbly above her head. Margret remembered Sonja singing to her guitar, and how the combination of gentleness and energy had taken her by surprise.

The next song had a faster beat, and the crowd spread out. The dancers disentangled and their movements took on more of an edge. They glanced off each other; Sonja too began to jump and pogo about on the dance floor. The flashing artificial lights of red, yellow or blue made her face look now mask-like, now happy and relaxed.

It was the first time Margret had seen Sonja dance. It was also her first time in a beer hall with live music. She elbowed her way to the dance floor. In a small space Margret clumsily tapped her feet to the next song and lost her balance the moment she tried to move from her space. She wobbled, and other dancers caught her and laughed, while her apology in English was drowned by the music. She laughed back, surrendered all the more to the beat and melody, and felt an increasing lightness.

It was only in the early hours that she noticed how drenched her dress was, after the band had played the last song, they too dripping with sweat. Now they trudged off, exhausted, along the corridor into a side room, as roadies began to roll up cables and dismantle the instruments.

Over the course of the evening the dance floor had thinned out. Someone turned on the overhead lights, and the remaining dancers blinked and stared at one another in bewilderment as they only now recognised each other's faces. For a moment, even Sonja's face looked strange to Margret. She watched as Sonja's new friends scribbled their addresses on crumpled bits of paper, beer mats or discarded receipts, and Sonja wrote her own address in clear letters on a piece of paper that she pressed into the dark-haired girl's hand. The girl put the scrap of paper carefully in her bag and then hugged Sonja, swaying slightly. When Sonja turned to go, Margret waved goodbye to the girls; then they climbed the cellar stairs and stepped out into the street.

On the way back to their pension, Sonja walked tiredly beside Margret, who greeted the slowly awakening city, its streets still empty and quiet. They walked past a bakery giving off an aroma of warm rolls; in one house a blind went up and there appeared an old man who opened the window and coughed heartily; through the river haze flew birds, their squawks sounding very near. While she let her dress dry, Margret cheerfully surrendered to her exhaustion.

Later they slept until midday, got up at a leisurely pace, had breakfast and wandered to the castle. On the way, Sonja hooked her arm through Margret's, a gesture she repeated over the following days and which united them both until the evening of their journey home.

∽

An anxious time began. Every morning when Margret went to the letterbox she feared finding a letter from the school office revoking Sonja's admission to extended secondary school[†]. No letter came, but Margret's distrust remained; she knew others who had received such letters a day before the start of school, typed in flawless German.

Nevertheless, on the first day of the new term, Sonja and she left the apartment together.

In school, Margret ran into Martin on the way to the staffroom. They said a polite hello, feeling their way, uncertain; finally, Margret said that he had helped her greatly by listening, and thanked him;

Martin nodded and replied that things were better with his wife, and that he too had her to thank for this.

They went their separate ways in the staffroom, each to other colleagues. The atmosphere – Margret sensed it instantly – was strange, charged, and at the same time more open than usual after the summer holidays. Several teachers were talking in abnormally loud and excited voices about their problems with pupils, the ridiculously rigid education, about the inadequate textbooks and the time wasted through frequent roll calls and meetings. There reigned a hopeful tension, in contrast to the years of paralysis.

In the ensuing weeks, Margret noticed that she was not the only one avoiding the headmaster. Most people still lacked the courage to speak up at meetings, but the air in the school building seemed abuzz with words. At the same time, when she walked along the corridor during break time, sometimes she heard the peculiar laughter of some colleagues standing in a small group with the headmaster. He asked none of them into his office.

In spite of the altered mood, Margret taught without conviction. She did feel pleased with one or another pupil who showed a sharp mind, but it felt as though she had brought something inside her to an end and that her fight now lay elsewhere, in the moments when she talked with Sonja, went with her to exhibitions, lectures or for a glass of wine in the evening.

They never spoke about Hans during their evenings together. When he said goodbye to them at the living room door, he looked either pensive or gloomy; Margret was unsure which. Sebastian mostly stayed at home in the evening. All the same, when she and Sonja came back later, Margret always found them in different rooms.

This awkwardness seemed to characterise the distance between Hans and the children, the wariness between him and her. He avoided arguing with her, but the silence between them was incredibly hard to bear. Words were left hanging in the air. As soon as they began to talk, one misinterpreted word was enough to spark off a row, from which one of them immediately backed down. Both seemed to know and to fear what would happen otherwise.

Even though Hans's thoughts remained a mystery to her, Margret was now able to live alongside him without fear of swallowing too many pills again.

Sonja would probably never know, Margret reflected, that she thanked her for that, every day

Farewell

Hans • 1991

After reading the letter a week ago, Hans had carefully slipped it inside a compartment of his briefcase and thought: I won't need the briefcase for a while. What he had not thought was: ever again. Now, as he looked for a seat on the tram, the thought flashed through his head. In shock and disbelief, he made his way to a free window seat and sat down.

In the mornings these past few months there had been few people on the tram. Hans stared at the two seats over by the other window, with slashed upholstery and foam padding spilling out. Over one armrest someone had scrawled in thick black marker: "Red Socks out†". Although Hans had heard this phrase often lately – word for word, or a variation thereof – from youngsters in the street, the woman next door or a chorus of demonstrators on the television, a shiver went down his spine. On the armrest of the seat opposite he read: "Kohl is shit†", scrawled in similarly thick clumsy letters.

Hans knitted his brow. He liked the familiarity of the tram, the fir-green faux-leather upholstery (undamaged until now), the shrill ring, the grubby windowpanes; and anyway, these two phrases corresponded as little to each other as the deserted barracks on one side of the tramlines corresponded to the colourful cars on the other, half-on, half-off the pavement in a continuous row.

At the third stop, through the window Hans watched some petite women, barely older than him, one of whom was holding out her open shopping bag to the others. The women were bent over the bag in rapture. Hans pressed his worn briefcase tighter to his stomach. Here, on the other hand, was a clear correspondence: between the greed with which people now carried home their wares in oversized plastic bags, filled their apartments with them, discarded their old things, tried to forget; and the disconcerting call for a united Fatherland, which had first rung out two years ago in streets across the country and which had unsettled even Margret who, unlike him, came back at first from every pro-reform demonstration with a gleam of hope in her eyes.

Hans got out at the stop in the city centre, as he had for so many years, and strolled over to the herbarium. In the coming days he would still need his briefcase; but he would not take out the letter. He knew its contents by heart: of course they valued his scientific work, but his success was not solely attributable to his ability and application but as much to the privileges his function on the university party leadership board had earned him.

The letter was signed by the new rector, a well-known academic at the university. On the one hand, Hans had always admired this man's courage in working against the generally accepted opinion and in foregoing Party favour in his quest for knowledge, but on the other he had perceived it as disloyal.

Hans felt the same impotence that had followed his anger upon first reading the letter.

After exiting the pedestrian zone, he crossed the main road and trudged up the pavement. Behind him at the traffic lights cars screeched to a halt. He heard workmen shouting instructions or playful jibes to each other. Cranes swinging slowly over the town centre cut through the pristine blue of the sky. The road Hans now came to was lined with semi-derelict buildings covered in banners and graffiti, and a brightly painted café with young people sitting on the terrace.

Inside the herbarium, on the stairs to the first floor Hans made way for several men carrying writing desks with white laminate coating, dismantled sheets of chipboard, chairs with metal legs and thin, varnished wooden seats. He turned and watched as they loaded the furniture onto a bulk-waste lorry. The chairs looked old but undamaged, the same kind of chair Hans had over many years certainly felt the hardness of, but rarely complained about.

He carried on up to the first floor where some of his colleagues were standing in the corridor, smoking and chatting relaxedly as though they felt at home in the chaos. When he walked past and said hello, momentarily they stopped talking and returned his greeting.

During recent months Hans had often stood here with them to discuss things or to fill the time, now that no one knew what their job was.

Suddenly, letters had arrived from countless countries making offers to the herbarium staff, offers to send unidentified plant species (should the university grant the necessary funding), more durable labels, tweezers that were sturdier yet finer at the same time, boxes of card that showed the plants to greater advantage, and each week the biologists received new specifications for systematising the plants. In the end Hans and his colleagues had marked time and fled into the corridor.

After reading the letter, Hans had stubbornly told himself that he didn't want to work at the herbarium any longer anyway. He opened his office door and slipped in. The scent of jasmine was almost suffocating. Some of the thin tendrils had long overgrown the trellis and wound their way up long, thin canes to the top of the window frame and along it.

Hans sat at his desk and looked at the thick white clouds of star-shaped flowers, which presently would wilt and fall onto the windowsill, whilst at other points fresh ones would grow. With the back of his hand he swept into a small pile some flowers that had already withered and detached themselves. He studied them in his palm. They were yellowed and lustreless and had all but lost their fragrance. They crackled when Hans crushed them in his hand.

Scissors in hand, he purposefully climbed onto his desk and in various places severed the tendrils ranging horizontally along the window frame, so that they plummeted like shot birds. Then he tugged at the canes until they pulled free from the soil along with the shoots. He climbed down and for a moment contemplated the trellis. There was no room for it in their apartment. He walked over, was about to pull it out of the soil, then stood still.

His gaze glided over five thick grey binders on the shelf beside his desk. From his briefcase he pulled two nylon bags (which he had carefully folded, despite them being partly torn at the seams), lifted the first two binders and laboriously slipped the bags over them. Then he took a thin pile of books from the shelf and stowed them in his briefcase. Lastly, he opened the door a fraction and put his ear out to the corridor. It was unusually quiet, to his relief.

A nylon bag in his left hand, his briefcase and the other bag in his right, he carried the now-redundant work materials to the door. There he set them down to collect later, took a deep breath and opened the door wide.

He went to the window and clasped his arms around the jasmine plant pot. In the botanical garden below, one of the gardeners was digging a hole for a small sapling. He was forcing the newly delivered plants into tight spaces so that they would grow close together and have to fight for nutrients. Hans knew that some of them would perish.

Gently he lifted the pot from the sill, so that the trellis did not wobble too much and topple over, carried it across the threshold and set it down in the corridor. After he had locked the door, he placed the key on the damp soil and lifted up the pot anew.

When he reached the end of the corridor, perspiring under the weight of the plant, an office door opened and a female colleague called, "Will you be back?"

Hans nodded as he continued, without turning round.

∽

On this hot June night the jasmine, whose fragrance had suffused the bedroom for a month now, looked to Hans like a shadowy figure on the sill behind the curtain.

As a child, so as not to fall asleep on the last six nights of the old year and the first six nights of the new, Hans had tossed and turned, believing he was to blame for his dreams and would, like an accomplice, receive his rightful punishment when a bad dream came true in the course of the year.

Now he tossed and turned because he could not get to sleep. A combination of the heat and his thoughts kept him awake. He was forty years older and had learned through countless dreams that they could make the nights unbearable, but all the same were not readily reenacted by day.

Suddenly he felt as though he were waking from a decades-long dream that had felt not unpleasant and for which he ought now to be punished. This dream was his life thus far, which, in spite of all the quarrels with Margret and the children, within a framework had readily gained meaning. This framework had been his country, which, unlike the neighbouring western one, had valued people, not money, and which had promised a future.

Hans's punishment was the loss of his job.

He remembered comrades who had been invited before the university party leadership to give public account of themselves, and his own unease which he had ignored time and again. While these comrades had tried to vindicate or at least explain themselves, Hans had usually stared at the floor, but always raised his hand in agreement when it came to deciding someone's expulsion from the Party.

Once, Hans had accompanied an injured young man to hospital in the party secretary's car and told the doctor it had been an accident. He could not remember whether someone had struck the man or whether he had smashed his own head against the top of his desk in despair. Whatever the case, he still saw clearly the man's bloodied forehead, his damaged face flat on the desk, hands lying motionless, and saw on the opposite side of the desk a row of men sitting together, of whom he had been one.

He recalled a woman who had applied for an exit visa and with head lowered had confessed to her "misdemeanour".

We needed every individual and no one could just leave when they felt like it: for years these words had sounded reasonable to Hans; he had been led to believe that it was like with children who had to learn certain rules, only these rules applied not to a small family but to an entire society.

Hans thought of Sonja, whose will he had been unable to direct by hitting her. Despite their estrangement he did not think of her as wayward, and although there were certain things about her he did not like – her dreaminess, her imprudence – on occasion he even found himself admiring her determination, though he was unwilling to admit it.

As he turned from one side onto the other, from his back onto his stomach, suddenly he sensed Margret moving too.

"Are you thinking about your work?" she asked him quietly.

Hans searched for words to express his thoughts. Finally he said, "It's hot and stuffy in here."

He kneeled on his pillow, drew aside the semi-opaque curtains and slid the jasmine over to the other side of the window. A few flowers detached themselves and fell onto the bed sheet. Neither he nor Margret brushed them off. For an instant their eyes met. Hans opened the window and wondered whether the jasmine tendrils would grow again.

"I'm not going to work at school any longer," he heard Margret say.

He turned around. Because he felt uncomfortable looking down at her, he slipped back under the covers.

"And what'll we live on?" he asked.

Margret's thoughts rang clearly, carefully considered, as she told him that she wanted to retrain; even though she ought to be glad because at long last her pupils were talking openly – at least, it seemed so to her. She explained that at first this had made her decision harder – because even before the momentous changes, she had been thinking of looking for a different job – but, strangely, she felt more fear now than before at the idea of having to educate children. When she met to talk with her colleagues in the staffroom, she sensed a slight suspicion, even amongst those who were friends; not the feeling of being spied on, like before – more a kind of marking of boundaries, which she thought was now spreading after a brief phase of great openness: first the obligatory, often hypocritical "we", then a time of strange frankness, and now the predominance of "me". Everyone had become more formal and their conversational topics were different; she herself had only ever spoken about personal matters with one or two colleagues, but now even Martin talked almost exclusively about his house, which he and his wife were intending to buy. "Sometimes," Margret said, "I visualise the children in ten, fifteen years, and I don't think I'll be able to do anything for them any longer." She was silent for a time. Eventually she said, "But for a sick person, say, I could."

"You'll have colleagues at a hospital too," Hans said.

"I won't have to educate them," Margret replied, and after a pause she continued, "Perhaps your father could've been cured now."

"No," said Hans, "I don't think so."

He could not recall when they had last lain so close together and spoken thus. All that Margret had said about her colleagues went through his head. He would need time to understand it.

As Margret pulled back the covers and stood up, in the streetlamp glow Hans saw her thin, faded nightdress, her nipples showing through, goose pimples on her forearms. She shut the window, slid the heavy plant pot back across – again some petals fell without a sound – and drew the curtains again.

Hans asked himself whether her hair was still blonde or had already turned grey. He would have liked to ask her to let it grow again. Had she noticed that his hair had gradually thinned and long since lost its black colour?

Timidly he touched her hair. It felt thick and strong. Margret lay on her back with her eyes closed and surrendered to the gesture.

"I wonder what Sonja's doing just now?" she asked in a tired voice.

"She'll be asleep," Hans replied.

But he was not sure. He pictured her dancing in a discotheque and thought of the foreign language, the French alcohol, hashish, fast music, men… Did she perhaps have a boyfriend neither he nor Margret knew anything about and who stayed with her? In the evening did she go swimming in the sea with her girlfriends? After all, Marseille was ten degrees warmer than here, she had written once.

"Everything's gone so fast," he said. "Until recently, that city she lives in," and he traced a wide circle with his arms, "was out of reach for us."

"Yes," Margret replied. "I hope she comes back."

Hans got up. His back and knees ached slightly. He walked through the living room without turning on the light and carefully opened Sebastian's door. Inside, he clicked on the desk lamp and sat down on the bed edge. He studied Sebastian's pale face, his stubble, his dark hair and lovely arched eyebrows.

How they had argued last year, when Sebastian had announced that he wanted to study economics and later earn decent money, perhaps even buy a house.

"There's nothing to study here," Hans had replied in irritation, "Your mother and I, we already know everything about this country. I can teach you it myself."

"But, Father, just look around you," Sebastian had said.

Angrily, Hans had stepped over to his son. "You're conforming."

"Like you, Father, your whole life long," Sebastian retorted, without stepping away.

Hans had sunk into a chair. "I'm a conformist, I know." he said quietly.

"For me you are a father who works, keeps quiet or argues." With these words Sebastian had walked out of the room, shutting the door almost inaudibly.

Well, that's the work over now, Hans thought. But could he not have read Sebastian animal stories or adventure books at bedtime when he was young, asked him just once where his interests lay? The boy he was looking at was grown up, taller than Hans by half a head when they stood face to face, so that Hans always had to look up to him a little now. But because Sebastian was less intransigent, less categorical than Sonja when showing his affections or challenging him, plus he did not want to move away from the city, possibly they could enjoy an evening in the pub like pals now and then. Hans brushed his hand over the foot of the cool bedcover; more, he did not dare.

When he went back into the bedroom, Margret appeared to be asleep. He lay down beside her.

A shrill ringing roused him in the morning. As with surprise he wondered at the unexpected dearth of dreams over the past hours, Margret slipped out of bed and ran to the telephone. Several minutes later she came back. Hans looked at her and could spot no grey in her hair.

"Your mother fell down the stairs last night," Margret said to him, in an almost accusatory tone. "A neighbour found her early this morning. She was unconscious."

৪৩

Lene was sitting on the narrow bench under the shed's shade-giving eaves, wiping her forehead with a handkerchief. After a while she felt for her skirt pocket and put her hankie inside. As she did, her eyes rested on the last of the redcurrant bushes. She rubbed her hand several times over the rough wood of the bench, against which her walking stick with the old plain handle leaned carelessly at an angle, within easy reach.

Hans opened a dormer window and wiped the sweat from his forehead. From up here his mother looked small. He leaned a little out of the window and let his gaze wander over the old rabbit stall, then over Lene again, the shed, and away up over the uncut lawn to the garden gate. He knew Lene would be unable to see him, even were she to look up now.

No matter who the buyer was, in a few years Hans would not recognise the house. Already the dark-grey slates on the roof were starting to come off, cracks showed in the stone floor of the laundry room, the dry closet next door smelled of sewage, the stovepipes in the kitchen and top room were corroding, and paint was peeling off the doors.

In a partition of the attic space, Hans stacked the slightly damp firewood in boxes and crates. They smelled familiar, like the entire attic. Carefully Hans carried the firewood down the smooth stairs and set down box after box, crate after crate in the yard. The neighbour would collect them later.

Lene had pithily decreed who should get which items of furniture, kitchen utensils, bath, dish and hand towels, tin bowls, pots, pans, crocheted blankets, clothes and shoes, crockery and cutlery, and had been surprised to find that most villagers and relatives declined her offers.

Not long ago the village *Konsum* next to the school had shut, and a small supermarket opened in the same building. Some things – toys and clothing – that had once filled an entire floor of the *Konsum* were no longer sold in the supermarket. Hans remembered Lene's bemused shake of the head when she offered one of her coats to a younger woman from the village, and the woman had waved aside her offer with a smile: "Thanks, Lene; I'll pop into town later and buy myself something nice."

After Hans had deposited all the boxes and crates in the yard, he sat down at the end of the bench beside his mother. He saw the swollen elbow on her thin right arm. Violet-yellow blotches showed on her wrinkled skin. Lene had recovered from her fall quicker than a woman her age might have been expected to. Hans studied her walking stick and noticed how worn around the edges the old handle was.

"The two boxes with my things are in the bedroom," Lene said, as she smoothed her overall over her soft stomach and thighs. She had at once known what she wanted to take with her, as though she had already thought long about it: three cardigans bought once in the *Konsum*, a woollen winter coat, three knee-length skirts, two thin blouses and one warm one, her Sunday dress with the pearl buttons; house shoes, boots, loafers, sandals (a pair of each); two pairs of tights; underwear; two hair combs, a magnifying glass, a few puzzle books, the gold-plated alarm clock with the big numerals; no knitting, no secateurs, no photos, no letters.

"The children always ran around here and kicked the ball against the fence," she said, and with her walking stick traced an arc over the lawn to the neighbour's fence, without following it with her eyes. Hans tried to imagine how Lene saw her garden in blurred colours. He blinked in the sun and his eyes strayed to the last remaining currant bush, dripping with golden-green and translucent red berries which he would perhaps yet gather.

"Just before I scythed the grass, it was always so high that they preferred to play hide-and-seek," Lene added.

Once the children were bigger, Hans had paid a strong competent man from the neighbourhood to tend the lawn with a scythe and a lawnmower. Until the house sold, the man would continue to do so.

In the upper corner of the garden the boughs of a tall birch tree swayed in the wind. From behind the left wall of the shed protruded the branches of a young apple tree with an unusually large crown. Often Lene had told the story of the apple core that Sonja was said to have buried there.

"Your children and grandchildren could have had a nice life here," Hans heard. Only gradually did he realise that Lene was talking about his grandchildren. His eyes lingered on the sky again, almost achingly azure, as Sonja too had described in one of her letters. He could think of hardly any other similarities between his village and the city where Sonja lived just now.

He felt a curious pang, then his heart began to beat faster: his life could yet be of use; he would prove it to Sonja and Sebastian by treating their children with affection, by granting them the innumerable hours of attention he had denied his own children. Calm and relaxed, he could play for hours with them at shops, football, cake-baking and puppets, rock a doll's crib for a girl, build a train track for a boy.

But when Hans thought of the toyshop windows he grew uneasy. How would he cope if his grandchild insisted on dragging him into a toyshop, pleading for a monster or a warplane? He was not keen on them, these olive-green, black and blue monsters with eyes narrowed ready for war, toned muscular bodies, swords, truncheons or rockets, clad in armour like advancing warriors, positioned next to army vehicles with in-built battle stations.

He asked himself when these toys had first appeared and whether he had failed to notice them before. These shop-window warriors horrified him, whereas the real tanks that day after day had trundled out of the barrack gates opposite their apartment had never frightened him.

A car hooting at the rear gate interrupted his thoughts.

"The taxi," Lene said, and felt for her walking stick.

Hans accompanied her to the gate, where the taxi driver took her arm. Then he went back to the house and into his parents' chilly bedroom. The smell from the old wardrobe of unworn, long-stored clothes still lingered in the air, and, when he inhaled deeply, Hans even caught Lene's body smell. He cast a final glance at the picture of the shepherd and his flock before lifting up a box and carrying it to the taxi. He fetched the second box without looking round.

He and the driver loaded the boxes into the spacious boot. Then Hans pulled the garden gate to, reached through the two wooden fence posts for the rusty bolt, slid it across and looped the rope tied to the top of the gate over the nearest post.

He walked over to the taxi. Lene was staring through the windscreen, down the road to the village exit. Hans half turned again and briefly raised his right hand, palm towards the house; but when he saw the taxi driver looking at him he quickly made the gesture into an explanatory one by pointing to the house next door and telling the driver that someone interested in buying his mother's house lived there.

Hans opened the back door of the taxi and got in.

∞

The nursing home in the district town was a broad, two-storied seventies building with pale paintwork, small windows and a flat roof.

Margret and Hans walked through reception and down the corridor to where the residents' area began. Between them they were carrying a holdall, gently leaning on each other, their backs bowed.

When they entered Lene's room, she peered over with vacant eyes and gazed just past them. However often Hans visited her here, every time he thought: a hospital room for a virtually blind old woman, whose eyes cannot be healed or even treated.

Lene was sitting at the small square table in the middle of the room, magnifying glass in hand, poring over a puzzle book as she made inaudible sounds through her lips. Hans bent down to her, momentarily pressed her head against his shoulder and then walked to the window. Outside, the driver of a dirt-splattered digger was loading a trailer with indiscriminately scattered tubes, rusty pipes, wires and unwieldy rocks mixed with sand and earth. One dirty white cellar wall of the neighbouring building was still standing solidly in the ground at the edge of the building site. Two nursing homes side by side, how about that then? the manager of the home had said to Hans once, in passing; still, he'd be happy, if only the visitors would stop fighting over the few parking places.

"Doesn't bother me, the noise," Hans heard Lene say behind him. "I'm awake at five every morning anyway."

He turned away from the window and noticed Lene had her cardigan buttoned right up. It was the end of August. Before, when she still lived in her house, she had worn only a thin pullover or blouse under her overall, whatever the time of year.

Margret bustled around the room. After placing the shampoo bottles in the bathroom and storing the juice cartons, tins of fish and sausage in Lene's cupboard, she took a cake parcel from the bag and laid it on the table beside Lene's puzzle book. Lene raised her chin and fumbled for the cake; her hand brushed the sticky paper through which orange-coloured filling glimmered. Before Hans could decide if he should tell her not to touch it, Lene withdrew her fingers, shut her puzzle book and pushed it to the table edge with the palm of her hand. She seemed to know the sequence of events for visits.

As she sat there motionless in her chair, staring at the table in front of her without taking in the cloth pattern, Hans failed to understand how he could have been afraid of her as a child and a teenager and occasionally later on, too. He paced up and down as Margret laid the table with crockery borrowed from the home's kitchen. She stopped for a moment and spun around, as she did on every visit; her gaze wandered over the bed, spread with white linen, the bedside cabinet, the table, television and wardrobe, and quietly she exclaimed, "What a joy, a single room!"

The coffee from the thermos flask they had brought had a bitter aroma. Margret divided out the cake onto three plates and said to Lene, "You must take something, but most importantly your medicine."

And, as though in her own apartment, Margret went to the cabinet, studied one pill packet after another and finally took out a plastic tablet tray inscribed with the words: morning, midday, afternoon and night, two pills. In the adjoining bathroom she filled a tumbler with water. Lene held out her cupped hand as Margret came to her side.

"First take a sip of water, then swallow the pills, then rinse," Margret said to her.

Hans saw the irritation on his mother's face as she groped for the pills.

"Water first," Margret repeated, "and don't spill any."

She held the tumbler to Lene's chapped, pale red lips, and Lene grasped it surprisingly firmly. Again Hans was undecided as to whether he should intervene. He could not read Lene's thoughts, as passively she followed Margret's instructions.

Lene left her cake untouched. She gave brief, amiable answers to Hans's or Margret's questions about the weather, her clothing needs, the other residents, how well the nurses were caring for her.

Later Margret cleared the table and rinsed the crockery under running water in the bathroom, leaving the door ajar. Hans led his mother (who got up with difficulty from her seat) to the bed, sat beside her on the edge and pressed together his fingertips. He glanced at Margret's slender figure in the bathroom, then regarded Lene.

Week by week his mother had shed the fat from around her stomach, and now, less carefully dressed in woollen leggings and cardigan, her bottom appeared flat, her hips narrow without their former flesh, her thighs almost skeletal. Hans could not help but notice that, before the move, her body muscle had been reducing because she hardly ever worked in the garden and because the neighbour carried the coal from the cellar for her, the firewood down from the attic. Now, though, she seemed to be steadily shrinking, as though her person were further diminishing the less active she became, as though she were physically replicating her sense of redundancy. Hans had presumed she would be glad to be looked after, to no longer have to wash the floor on her knees, cook lunch only for herself and keep the house tidy.

"I still think about my flowers," Lene said softly, and inclined her head familiarly towards Hans. "The fragrant roses, the red chrysanthemums, the asters I cut for Erwin's grave."

"And I often think of the potato harvest," said Hans. "The milking and the scything."

"You were always able," Lene said.

Hans lifted his head and studied his mother's profile, her now almost shapeless face and her white, badly cut hair under the net.

"Afraid, I was," he murmured.

Margret gave a jolt; she half turned round, but continued with the washing, whereas it seemed Lene had heard nothing.

As if under duress, Hans began to talk about before: about the farm, the garden and the minister, the chimney and the food; Lene listened and contradicted him and told her version, one minute shaking her head in surprise, the next nodding in agreement. Every so often they would laugh, then argue again until one of them backed down in abeyance or conciliation. They fell silent when Margret suddenly stood before them with the empty bag and asked what things she should bring on their next visit.

On their way out, as Hans stooped to briefly hug Lene, she whispered, "Please, I'd like to have Erwin's grave near."

∞

Several weeks later, Hans returned from his first visit to the job centre, a thin bundle of papers in his briefcase. The first deep-red leaves of autumn were blazing on a vinegar tree on the short slope behind their apartment block. It still felt balmy, like summer; the air smelled of exhaust fumes, also of washing powder, thanks to the blouses, trousers and underwear that flapped in the light breeze on the drying green; every week, new garments could be found on the lines that stretched from pole to pole. High up on the hillsides, the air must be fragrant from fermenting fruit, thought Hans.

He tucked his briefcase between his knees, opened the letterbox and picked out the newspaper, some flyers and a letter from Sonja: the first for weeks. Relieved, he put it between the newspaper and flyers and went up.

As he was unlocking the apartment door, he debated whether to read the letter straight away or wait until Margret came home in the afternoon. She currently spent her weekdays in a room with other adults, where once again she sat on one of two hard seats behind a school desk, taking notes, attentively following what the tutor said, though not without checking.

Hans went into the kitchen, impatiently picked up a spoon and started to insert the handle through a small hole at one corner of the envelope. He stopped, laid the spoon on the counter and took some scissors from the next drawer to slit open the envelope without damaging it.

Then he read standing, smiling to himself and endeavouring to understand every word Sonja had written in uneven handwriting. Near the end of the letter her writing became messier. Hans's contentment turned to consternation when he realised from the final lines that Sonja was expecting a baby with a French man and had no immediate plans to return to Germany.

He slipped onto the kitchen stool. Again he saw Sonja before him, by the sea, slim to start with, then with a bump under her swimsuit, later with the infant in a pram as she weaved through lanes of hooting cars, or sat in a park and talked with other mothers while she fed the baby on a bench beside a small pond, with the background noise of buses and the occasional plane coming in to land or taking off over the city. With regret he thought that Margret and he would be unable to understand a word of their conversation.

And Sonja's face: how should he visualise it now, in her third month of pregnancy? Happy, relaxed, even with a delicate, contented smile, or gripped by the fear of what was to come, pensive or despairing? Or pale from the strains of the first months, the exhaustion, the sickness, the sudden fluctuation in her hormones? Hans knew little about all that; what he had pieced together he had either read in books or overheard from women talking on the tram. He could not recall how Margret had been during her pregnancies, nor had he asked her about it afterwards.

Hans put the letter in the envelope with care, carried it to the living room and placed it in the middle of the dinner table. When Margret came home she would see it at once.

∞

It was still light when later that day Hans and Margret took the tram north, to the stop close to the city exit sign, from where, if you followed a narrow lane left, you reached the farm where they had once got to know each other.

They got out of the tram, turned right and walked side by side at the edge of a quiet road, slowly, sedately, silently. As yet there were no curled dried leaves at the roadside for the wind to carry across the road. Along the fields trundled two tractors, one pulling a potato harvester that dug into grey-brown furrows, the other driving alongside with a virtually full trailer connected to the harvester by a conveyor belt. Hans thought of the heavy baskets of potatoes they had hauled over the fields on their placement. Now he watched as the wilted plants, cut by an unseen part of the machine, fell back down to earth and moments later potatoes appeared in the harvester, free from stones, earth and any remaining weed, to then be rolled across into the trailer.

"I knew so little about your childhood," Margret said suddenly, as the noise of the harvester gradually faded. The road now turned and led to the next village, to a small church of light stone showing signs of wear without diminishing its beauty.

199

Hans regarded Margret's face in the early autumn light. "I know next to nothing about yours," he responded.

They followed the rise in the road that, for the next kilometre, became a link road between two villages. At the bottom of an incline grew apple and sweet cherry trees; their branches still bore some black, partly withered fruit. As Margret walked on, Hans reached up to a lower branch and picked one of the autumn apples, which he rubbed clean on his windcheater. He knew Margret was particularly fond of their sharp taste and carried on briskly up the road.

Margret took the apple as a matter of course, thanked him and bit into it. Hans smelled the bright fruity flesh. She turned to him, and he stood next to her so that together they could look back at the cityscape, the tranquil river, the hills of green dotted with the first hints of autumn. They gazed at the city centre and the university tower that outreached even the tallest cranes, at nearby fields and the village church.

Perhaps they would soon tear down the tower, completed not long after Sonja's birth. Strange, thought Hans, how you can get used even to ugly things, so much so that you wouldn't wish to be without them.

"I always thought I would take the same route with our grandchildren as I did with our children," Margret said, turning round thoughtfully.

Although it was already dusk, they wandered farther along the road that soon petered out into an unlit gravel track, once more lined by fields. Hans thought of his mother, who would probably never again be able to tread such uneven paths, and of their unborn grandchild who would first have to learn to walk.

Hans trod with care, trying to avoid the deepest ruts. Despite the developing darkness, the cloudy sky gave off a certain glow. Hans pointed the way to Margret, who carefully followed him, and when she almost slipped he automatically grabbed her arm and momentarily held it tight. Silence surrounded them, broken by the sound of their footsteps, of the breeze as it blew through the sparse trees, an occasional rustle in the fields, the murmur of the city in the distance. But Hans sensed this was a different, more hopeful silence than their oppressive poverty of words over recent years.

Thus they reached the next village and came to a poorly lit area that they crossed to reach a main road leading back to the city. Kilometre after kilometre they walked one behind the other at the roadside, blinded by the lights of oncoming cars.

Beyond the city entrance sign they sat down at last on a chilly metal bench under the new roof of a tram shelter and drank tea from their flask, stained brown on the inside. Hans refused when Margret offered him a sandwich because he did not feel hungry; however, he agreed to her suggestion that they go the rest of the way on foot and forego the tram.

The street lights cast a cold light on the pavement. An older, yellow tram passed with a soft screech. They turned off the main road and came to a neighbourhood with fifties-built blocks like their own, with piles of rubbish lying outside: bulk waste – a light-coloured desk, a cooker, ripped seats, a wooden stool, mattresses, a music system – mixed with a residue of carpets and fabrics, books, shoes, food waste, cartons and bags. Hans surveyed the rubbish in the light of the streetlamps. Protected by rows of housing and hills, he no longer felt the wind.

Margret too examined all the rubbish as she slowly walked past, before stooping over a mountain of books illuminated by a flickering streetlamp. She bent down and tried to read the titles and publisher, then piled the books on the flat step in front of the door. Suddenly she stopped, leafed through a tattered book and said dully, "By my father."

She thrust her hands deeper into the pile of discarded books and extracted two more which, after a brief browse, she added to the pile. Opening the first book she had found, she walked to the curb and waited for the streetlamp to cast a steady light. Then she read in a loud voice: "Because generations are always the offspring of all fathers and mothers. Generations also precede generations. If the generational problem in literature – and we will need to speak about this shortly – is often portrayed as a family problem, nevertheless, in the historical reality it is always more than merely a family problem; it is therefore ultimately – and this applies particularly to our today – a question of class; for history, insofar as we are able to retrace it in written evidence, has been the history of class struggles." She smiled dubiously, slid her fingers down the margins and eventually placed the book on top of the others.

Almost inaudibly she said into the night, "Will we go and visit Sonja once her baby's been born?"

Hans nodded, without knowing whether Margret saw.

∞

Winter arrived with unusual severity; Lene's village was snowed in. Hans was glad his mother no longer lived there. Every day, he and the neighbour shovelled a path through metre-high drifts from the garden gate to the house so that all house viewings could be kept. Most viewers left non-committally after a quick tour, and, when the snowdrifts thinned, Hans and the neighbour drove Erwin's gravestone and urn over to the cemetery of the district town. It was a simple rectangular treeless space enclosed by a pale stone wall, not far from the nursing home, as Lene had wished. Hans was unfamiliar with the names of the dead.

A few weeks later, on the graves and headstones here and there lingered only uneven patches of snow, greyish at the edges. Margret was on her haunches with a trowel, digging holes in which she placed white crocuses and dark-red primulas. She pressed the soil firmly around the flowers. Then she brushed the damp earth from her hands, scrunched up the bag she had brought the plants in and stood up.

As they walked towards the rubbish bins, Hans read over and over the two names engraved on the gravestone and the dates underneath.

This is how he knew it from his village: people did not die in winter but in spring, once they had come through the hard period and could breathe again. And had not Lene lost this rhythm in the home? Or had she felt no need to gather her energy, so that over the course of the winter she went into gradual decline, sitting on her bed hour after hour, unable to see the sense in eating and drinking, walking and sleeping, in all activity?

Hans was unsure.

On Boxing Day, when he and Margret visited with dumplings, red cabbage and the remains of the Christmas goose, Lene had sat absently in her chair and with an adamant shake of her head refused to put on her Sunday dress. Later, with lips firmly pressed, she had refused her food until Margret, who was trying to feed her, in the end let fall the violet cabbage from the fork onto Lene's trousers. Lene sat motionless and waited serenely until the stain was removed. Only at the end of the meal did her eyes light up as she told them she had finally remembered the second verse and then begun to sing a song in a hoarse voice, "*Then mine eyes fill with tears / my heart with sweet sorrow / farewell... farewell... farewell...**"

When she returned to herself – the end of the verse seemed to elude her – Lene had continued to hum the melody, and had given a start when Hans indicated to Margret not to clear up just yet. When they said goodbye he hugged his mother as briefly as always.

Lene Gräf and Erwin Gräf: the names of his parents, plain and unadorned, one under the other. Their surname was also his own, and that of Margret. In two weeks the crocuses would fade. In ten years the stone would be removed.

In Hans's mind the pictures would live on until his death.

On the Horizon

Sonja • 1992

Sonja looked out at the line that separated sky and sea. She had yet to travel to Africa, the continent that began far out there, where water eventually met land.

Supported by her hands, she sat reclined on her jacket, which she had spread out on one of the breakers formed of limestone rock that lined the shore not far from the beach. Several hundred metres behind her ran the Marseille coast road, from whence came the incessant roar of traffic, while before her lay the sea, quiet and all but still, its surface gently rippling.

In Germany at the beginning of March it had never been warm enough outside for her to be without her jacket. Some of the colourful patterned material trailed over the rock, and from a pocket peeped a piece of paper – her parents' last letter: had Sonja, barely turned twenty, wanted the baby? Did she now intend to stay there for good? Could her parents come to visit?

Gazing anew at the strangely clear line on the horizon, Sonja ran her hands over her bump several times.

She had already replied to her parents: yes, she had wanted the baby; they would be welcome to visit; whether she would stay here for good, though, she did not know.

The baby could no longer turn in the restricted space of her stomach without kicking or gently punching. The sea stirred, and a light wind sent small waves onto the beach as Sonja sensed her baby's movements: not the patting of her early pregnancy, no – now the baby was fighting for more space.

Sonja closed her eyes and raised her head.

She saw her parents in the living room, standing face to face, her father with black hair, her mother blonde, in front of the already drawn curtains, while out on the army barracks Soviet soldiers sang to accordion accompaniment. Her parents' shouting had drowned out the soldiers' song.

She had been eight years old at the time, a skinny girl with short, tomboyish hair, and had got up to go to the bathroom. Her parents seemed not to notice their daughter standing in the doorway. Although Sonja had been frightened by the manner in which they glared at each other, it was only when her father raised his hand to her mother that she had retreated to her room.

Over many evenings from her bedroom Sonja had listened to her parents' relentless heated exchanges and got up to repeatedly witness them standing face to face, pitilessly staring daggers at each other.

∞

Sonja opened her eyes. Over there, the unknown continent. Had there not once been the search for *Innermost Africa**, long before she, like her friends, left the city she knew so well?

Her father had followed the news on the television day by day as though paralysed, whilst her mother, amid throngs of people in the big inner-city square, had remained silent (not without hope) as they chanted that they were the people; meanwhile, Sonja and her friends, when not demonstrating themselves, would sit together every day after class in passionate debate to find suitable words for their plays and appeals, which they would direct at the people of their city and thereby furnish them with quotes and suggestions as to where things could go from here in schools, offices and factories:

As long as we believe in our future, we need not fear our past*.

The thing that may stifle us: to move from time in motion to time standing still*.

Suddenly *a warmer country** had seemed so near, even though it was coming on for winter.

Later, the demonstrators at the square had shouted staccato-like that they were *one* people, and Sonja's mother, sweating and seized by nausea, searched for a way to the edge of the crowd as people waved beer bottles and whistled each time someone announced themselves over the microphone as a comrade.

"If only we could talk normally with one other!" her mother had once said after coming home from a demonstration, and Sonja was unsure whether she had meant the people at the square, or herself and Sonja's father.

She might also have been referring to Sonja and her friends, had Sonja ever told her how they were suddenly no longer able to put down on paper words that matched their ideas: a misplaced comma, a nuance in meaning could all at once lead to long debate, at the end of which everyone drifted off, disgruntled. At first they still argued with each other, no one giving ground, but their discussions gradually gave way to a pedestrian exchange of opinions: time standing still. From meeting to meeting their silences grew; they looked at each other less and less, fingered their wine glasses with heads lowered and said nothing. Until the day came when one of them announced into the oppressive silence in a clear voice that he had recently booked a flight because in Africa, the real Africa, there were things to do other than have risible discussions about words. Sonja lifted her head and thought: there's not a thing for you to do there. But as she looked at the others' shocked faces, the friend had gazed dreamily out of the window and murmured, "And the warmth, you know…"

Not long after that, one by one the circle of friends had disbanded, and Sonja, who had no wish to be last, wondered with a shiver where she would go.

∾

Ever since the baby had started to grow inside her, Sonja no longer felt cold. Despite the wind, which was now blowing stronger, she removed her shoes and socks and burrowed her bare soles against the warm rock. She would have liked to climb down to the shore to paddle a little in the water but, being less agile because of her bump, was scared she might slip on the smooth stones and be unable to catch herself.

She glanced sideways at the jagged limestone rocks, virtually devoid of vegetation, which bore no resemblance to the hills of her city of birth.

When she arrived here over a year ago, at first the great French city had aroused her loathing because it was dirty and noisy from cars and buses hooting and harrying in close proximity to the sea, because its streets seemed endless, and because the parks, where you could retreat for a while, were scattered at inordinate intervals across town. All the same, Sonja had not gone back.

One evening a few days before she left her home city – she had still been living with her parents – Sonja had come back from the cinema, quietly opened the apartment door and entered without her parents noticing. As before, she stood in the living room doorway and watched them.

Her father was holding her mother's hands in his as he looked down diffidently and said almost inaudibly, "My dear Margret."

He seemed unsure of himself, afraid almost, as with a smile her mother slowly freed her hands from his and patted him on the shoulder like a friend.

Incredulous, and sensing she was witness to an intimate scene, Sonja had slipped from the room and gone to bed, but had been unable to sleep.

In the years leading up to the momentous changes, her parents' arguments had given way to mutual indifference. Although they no longer berated each other, they certainly did not touch one another; never had Sonja heard them speak to each other with affection.

Perhaps everything will make sense at a distance, Sonja had concluded.

∞

To her right, where the white pebble beach ran, several children were charging in Sonja's direction, now on the dry, chalky stones, now with their feet in the water. Sonja would come here again after the birth because it was somewhere children could play freely, away from the busy roads; not an entirely quiet place but peaceful all the same, and also good to retreat to after a heated row with Laurent.

Even though the baby had been kicking incessantly against her abdominal wall for a while, only now for the first time did Sonja feel a slight pain on the right, next to her navel. Did her baby sense her deep concern – despite the fact that she had not spoken or moved – that not a day passed without a fight with Laurent, with whom she intended to raise her child?

The children on the beach, perhaps six or seven years old, were now playing nearby, endeavouring to shape the gravelly sand into castles and ramparts which, without stability or foundation, instantly collapsed. Next, they started to go over their calves and feet with little chalk stones, as if trying to draw. When they only made red marks appear, they threw their stones into the water with loud cries and competed to see whose stone flew farthest.

Sonja tried to visualise her own child playing with other children a few years hence. She was unable to put a face to the unborn child; instead, she saw herself, her now-adult self, as though cut out of earlier photographs and placed in another setting.

She took one more look at the line, which might have been sky blue or sea blue. Then she slipped on her socks and shoes, carefully stood up and briefly clasped her hands under her belly, before turning her back to the sea and beginning to pick her way towards the coast road over stones that gradually grew flatter.

∞

Sonja's father got out of the train first and set down two suitcases, one after the other, on the platform. Then he lifted off the picnic bag, so familiar to Sonja, as were the two blue-and-burgundy checked cases used on every family holiday. She now saw her mother, who stepped carefully from the train and reached out her hand to her father for the last, high step.

Her parents seemed small and frail as they looked around for her. Sonja had only ever known her father with glasses, whereas her mother's were new, the lenses thinner than his.

Past her parents streamed businesspeople pulling cases, young people with rucksacks, one or two women with prams. These other people moved ahead with purpose, leaving her parents looking helpless and rather unworldly.

Sonja all but ran to them, her arms clasped round Gustave so that he did not bob about too violently in his sling. Breathless, she hugged her mother, who was now a head shorter than her. She shook her father's hand before slipping the white hat from Gustave's forehead and turning him so that her parents could see one side of his face. Her father beamed unreservedly, like a child. Sonja had never seen him smile like this. Beads of sweat glistened on his forehead, and when he wiped it with his cotton handkerchief, from the corner of her eye Sonja saw two young girls giggle as they looked on. She saw her father's thin grey hair and thought that probably you would never find paper tissues in his pockets.

Eventually her father picked up the cases. They went down the escalator, and while they waited for the metro, Gustave briefly opened his eyes, only to fall asleep again a moment later.

&

Inside the cool, quiet spacious hallway of the turn-of-the-century apartment building, they all breathed a sigh of relief. Sonja felt as though the heavy front door completely cut her off from the noise of the street and the sun-warmed air, a sensation she was familiar with and which increased the longer she had been outside. As they climbed up, however, the coolness evaporated, and when they entered the attic apartment she was glad to be able to undo Gustave from his sling.

Her parents had said in their letter that they would rather stay with Sonja than in a hotel, if there were somewhere for them to sleep. Inside the apartment they went over to Laurent, who got up from one of two writing desks in the main room and shook his hand with friendly reserve and a clumsy "*Bonjour*". Sonja translated the usual pleasantries as Laurent asked her parents about their journey, and they in turn thanked him for asking, and for his welcome.

While her mother disappeared into the spare room, her father sat down tiredly on a chair at the dinner table. Apparently glad of the break from his work, Laurent took the little one from Sonja, laid him on a blanket, bent over him and removed his thin cotton jacket and romper. Flexing his bare legs and arms, Gustave smiled back sweetly as Laurent laughed and made faces. As he changed the nappy with practised hands, Sonja's father looked on with interest. From time to time he lowered his head with a faraway look. His light shirt showed patches of sweat at the back.

Later, as Laurent prepared dinner, Sonja breast-fed Gustave on the couch. Her mother stole a glance at them as she went to the bathroom. Sonja remembered an evening a few weeks before her leaving exams, when her mother had explained to her why she had not breast-fed her; Sonja had been ill after her birth, and her mother had only been allowed to visit her in the clinic once a day.

∓

It was getting dark, and Gustave had been crying for a while. Weary from the journey and unused to the climate, Sonja's parents were sitting with Laurent at the dinner table. Her father had his hand on top of her mother's. The skin on the back was chapped. Sonja moved around with Gustave in his sling, murmuring in his ear. Her parents were silent, and occasionally smiled at Laurent; each time Sonja crossed the room, she saw that Laurent failed to return their smiles. After a time she undid the sling to pass the baby to her partner. Now he too paced the room but was likewise unable to quieten Gustave. When Sonja began to tie the sling again, her mother stepped over and asked if she could carry him for a while. For a moment there was silence; then, her father got up and asked the same question – urgently, almost pleadingly. Sonja avoided their gazes and refused, saying that she wanted to save them the bother after their tiring journey.

Even with the window open, the smell of dinner lingered: fish, olives and garlic. Suddenly her mother hurried into the spare room as if she had forgotten something important, and returned with a bottle of white wine, which she proudly positioned in the centre of the table, turning the modest, finely drawn label with the year to Laurent. He told her he was unfamiliar with the region, and although he politely thanked her, Sonja thought she detected an arrogance in his voice, as though he would think a wine from an unknown East German region could never be as good as one from the Alsace or the Loire. For a moment she felt torn between her origins, which Laurent made fun of, and her affection for him. Then her thoughts were interrupted by Gustave's piercing cries.

After Sonja's parents had gone to bed and Gustave had cried himself to sleep, Laurent sat at his desk again. Sonja stood beside him, following the French words as they appeared on the screen. At length she said that her mother had meant to please him with the wine. Laurent shrugged and said he still had some work to finish. Sonja retorted that he might try to communicate with her parents in English, her voice rising as she pleaded with him further, failing to hear his responses, whereupon Laurent's voice developed a sharp, defensive edge. They argued bitterly until a third voice joined in: a clear, strong voice. Together they hurried to the bedroom, bent over Gustave's cot and began to argue about who should take him, glaring angrily at each other across the cot.

Suddenly Sonja saw her still-dressed father in the doorway and fell silent. Without looking at Laurent she lifted Gustave, sat down with him on a chair and stared at the empty cot.

Gently her father asked to take the baby, saying that he had yet to hold him in his arms. He told them he had been unable to sleep for weeks now anyway. He looked back and forth between Sonja and Laurent.

Sonja pressed Gustave tighter to her stomach. Her father, now in the main room pacing up and down in his usual way, looked old and sad. After a moment she stood up, slowly walked over and handed him her child. Her father put his hands under Gustave's arms, brushing Sonja's fingers, and she felt the roughness of his skin. As she explained to him how to support the baby's head, she saw his mouth next to his little ear, and heard him whispering. Although Gustave cried, her father remained calm. Sonja felt a gentle tug in her stomach.

She had not noticed that her mother had also come into the room and was now asking Laurent in English if he still had a lot to do this evening. Laurent looked at Sonja sheepishly, then went over to the book shelves and unearthed a dictionary, which he placed next to the wine bottle. He looked at her mother and said no; with a wave of his hand he invited her to sit with him at the table. Hesitantly, in broken English, Laurent and her mother began to talk.

Sonja slid a stool under the kitchen window, sat down and, with one arm on the ledge, looked out into the night, up at the dark, cloudless sky. Tomorrow, she thought, they could all go to the spot on the beach where she had sat on the rocks a week before Gustave's birth. There should be days when the colours of the sky and the sea almost merge into one on the horizon.

My special thanks to:
Ursula Krechel, Bernd Henninger, Thomas Jung
and Michael Wildenhain

Glossary of Terms

Crèche the GDR provided state-run and -funded nurseries, which allowed up to 85% of women to work outside the home. Places were made available to all, free of charge, with parents only required to pay a nominal allowance for their children's meals.

East Zone after the Second World War, Germany was for several years governed by the four victorious allies of North America, the United Kingdom, the Soviet Union and France, each of whom occupied a territorial zone. On 1st July, 1945, the territories occupied by the three Western allies became formally separated from the Eastern, or Soviet Occupation Zone, which comprised the territory that in 1949 became the German Democratic Republic.

Extended Secondary School (EOS) a two-year preparatory school beyond secondary school for suitable university candidates. The threat of non-entry to EOS was used as an instrument of repression against those who refused to join the FDJ, or who had participated in *Junge Gemeinde* meetings, or been religiously confirmed.

Free German Youth originally founded in Germany in 1936 as an antifascist underground resistance movement, in the GDR it was run along Marxist-Leninist lines as the official youth movement of the SED for 14-25 year-olds. Although not obligatory to join, those who refused were often disadvantaged when it came to furthering their education and career. 77% of GDR 14-25 year olds were members in 1981. Most non-members declined on religious grounds. In German, *Freie Deutsche Jugend* is abbreviated to *FDJ*.

Free School Community an important German co-educational reform school, founded in 1906 in Wickersdorf, at the eastern edge of the Thuringia forest, which encouraged student-teacher autonomy and fostered camaraderie and leadership. It closed as an educational facility in 1991 and is today home to adults with special needs who live alongside able-bodied adults according to the principles of anthroposophy.

Gorbi Mikhail Gorbachev was the last leader of the Soviet Union (USSR), from 1985 until 1991. He promoted Glasnost (openness) and Perestroika (restructuring), policies which encouraged greater social and economic freedom, leading to liberalisation and an end to the monopoly of the USSR state Communist Party. In May 1989, a chain reaction was triggered across satellite Communist states in Europe, bringing about the rapid dissolution of the Eastern Bloc. When Gorbachev visited the GDR on 7th October 1989, to commemorate the nation's 40th anniversary, crowds chanted his name. Gorbachev was awarded the Nobel Peace Prize in 1990 in recognition of his pivotal role in a peaceful end to the Cold War.

Jugendweihe dating from the 19th Century, this secular coming-of-age ceremony for fourteen-year-olds marks entry into adulthood. In 1954 in the GDR the ceremony became a specifically socialist ritual, an atheist alternative to religious confirmation, whereby children pledged allegiance to the state's ideals and expressed international solidarity with other socialist nations. It would take place at the end of eighth grade to mark a pupil's progression from the *Young Pioneer* movement (specifically, Thälmann Pioneers) to the *Free German Youth*. Non-participation in the *Jugendweihe* could result in severe disadvantages for a child; as such, it was an important ideological instrument in the secularisation of GDR society.

Junge Gemeinde a Christian youth movement independent of GDR state influence and censorship where young people could freely air their views. Started as a peace movement in the 1960s, throughout the 1980s it increasingly became a focal point of anti-government resistance. In the GDR, churches in general played an important role as a place of peaceful protest, famously epitomised in the Monday demonstrations of the Leipzig churches, which began on 4th September 1989, and spread throughout the country in the lead-up to the fall of the Berlin Wall.

Kindergarten 98 per cent of GDR three- to six-year-olds attended kindergarten, with places provided to all free of charge.

Konsum consumer cooperatives were re-introduced to the Soviet Occupation Zone in 1946. In the GDR the word *Konsum* became a generic term for a grocer's shop. In 1959, GDR *Konsum* lettering was rebranded with the symbol "K" formed of an industrial chimney stack and a sickle.

LPG *Landwirtschaftliche Produktionsgenossenschaft* local farm cooperatives were part of the wider, industrial-scale, state-sanctioned collectivisation of agricultural production in the GDR.

Nationalpreis the National Prize of the GDR was awarded annually to people and groups for achievement in science, the arts, or other fields of merit. Winners were awarded in three classes and received a monetary prize, as well as a gold-plated medal. In 1971, one of the recipients was the famous GDR author, Anna Seghers, mentioned by surname near the beginning of the story.

The Party this capitalised noun refers to the Socialist Unity Party of Germany (SED), founded in 1946 with the merger of the German Communist Party (KPD) and the Social Democratic Party of Germany (SPD). The far-left leaning, Marxist-Leninist SED was the governing party of the GDR and held the monopoly on power from 1949 until 1989. The two principal leaders of the SED were Walter Ulbricht, from 1950 to 1971, and Erich Honecker, from 1971 until 1989. Where the word "comrade" appears in the novel, this generally indicates a person affiliated with the SED.

Politbüro the small inner circle of senior Party officers responsible for the day-to-day running of the SED's Central Committee.

Red Socks out/ Kohl is shit the first slogan was used to voice disapproval of East German citizens who formerly held a government-related role; the second to expressed discontent over German reunification and the new federal system of government. The two slogans ostensibly reflect political allegiance to either of the two principal opposition parties post reunification: the centre-right West German Christian Democratic Union (CDU), chaired by Helmut Kohl, eventually won a majority over the East German Party of Democratic Socialism (PDS), a reformed and liberalised version of the SED.

The 17th of June Uprising a significant revolt by East Berlin workers on 16th of June 1953, triggering mass anti-government protest which spread across the GDR the following day. The demonstrations were violently suppressed by the government, with the help of Soviet troops.

State Security the GDR secret police, commonly known as the Stasi (*Staatssicherheit*, State Security). Working closely with the Soviet KGB, it was a highly effective and repressive surveillance and spying organisation, consisting of full-time employees and unofficial informants, who were 'recruited' to spy on family, friends and neighbours. The Stasi infiltrated almost every aspect of GDR life. It is estimated that in total there was one informant for every 6.5 GDR citizens.

Trek after World War Two, Breslau came under Polish control again. The Polish authorities swiftly repopulated their former city, de-Germanising it by means of treks, or transports, of German refugees to elsewhere in Germany.

The Wall the Berlin Wall divided East and West Berlin from 13th August, 1961, until 9th November, 1989, and encircled West Berlin, creating a capitalist "island" within communist GDR. The Berlin Wall was separate to the much longer north–south inner German border, construction of which began in 1952.

War of Independence a famous painting by Swiss artist Ferdinand Hodler (1853-1918), *Students of Jena in the War of Independence, 1813*. Prussian forces combined with Russian, Austrian and Swedish troops to decisively defeat French Emperor Napoleon at the Battle of Leipzig, from 16th to 19th October 1813, in the largest battle pre-First World War, involving 600,000 soldiers.

Wehrmacht the unified armed forces of Nazi Germany under Adolf Hitler, in operation from 1935 until 1946 and closely aligned to the Waffen-SS, the paramilitary branch of the Nazi Party.

Wrocław the largest city in Lower Silesia, Poland, previously known as Breslau, was one of the foremost cities in Prussia and became a Nazi stronghold during World War Two. In August 1944, Hitler declared the city a military fortress to be defended against advancing Soviet Red Army troops. Breslau's fortress period lasted until 13th February 1945, when the Siege of Breslau began, ending in Red Army victory on 6th May. Breslau was the last major German city to surrender, two days before the end of World War Two. During the fortress period and subsequent siege, around 80 per cent of the city was destroyed. Many women were victims of rape, widely perpetrated by victorious Soviet soldiers.

Young Pioneers from first to third grade, school pupils were expected to join the *Young Pioneer* movement, which was an integral part of daily school life under the mantra that "a good school pupil is a good pioneer". Teachers greeted their class with the slogan "For peace and socialism – be prepared!" (shortened to "Be Prepared!") with the pupils' response being "Always Prepared!" The salute, imported from the Soviet Union, was five closed fingers representing the five continents, which must cooperate for future success; the raised hand symbolised collective interest over individual, "we" rather than "I", for the common goal of the victory of socialism. With ten socialist "commandments" for pupils to recite, the *Young Pioneers* was akin to a religious movement and designed to produce future socialist citizens and leaders.

From first to third grade, young pioneers wore a blue neckerchief;

from fourth until seventh grade they wore a red neckerchief and belonged to the Ernst Thälmann Pioneers. Thälmann was leader of the German Communist Party in the Weimar Republic and an idol of the GDR government. Once a month classes held a pioneer meeting, in which pupils assumed the various committee roles. Although not obligatory, those who did not join the Young Pioneers (or later the Thälmann Pioneers) could have difficulties at school. In 1989, 98% of GDR pupils were Young Pioneers.

Literary References

A warmer country a quote from the 1982 poem *The Innermost Africa* by Volker Braun (b. 1939), a famous second-generation GDR writer of plays, poetry, novels and short stories. As a writer he was critical of the regime, especially after the Prague Spring, and like many other writers sought through his work to change the system from within.

And the snowman... This is a line from a 2001 children's picture book by the famous West German storyteller, James Krüss, and refers to the words of a crow that reassures a snowman anxious about melting in spring that he will undergo three transformations, first melting, then flowing as water into the sea, before turning to water vapour, rising into the sky and falling again as snow in winter.

As long as we believe in our future a 1986 quote from Heiner Müller, the famous GDR playwright.

Bowed over the poppy Lines from a poem by Heinz Kahlau (1931-2012), one of the best-known poets in the GDR, a master pupil of Bertolt Brecht.

Far more flowers while we live / for they're no use on the grave A quote from a well-known poem by Austrian writer and poet Peter Rosegger (1843-1918) entitled *A little more Peace*.

Innermost Africa another quote from the 1982 Braun poem, *The Innermost Africa*

Kiki: The Story of a Dog a 1947 short story by the twentieth-century German doctor, writer and communist politician, Friedrich Wolf (1888-1953), who was exiled from Hitler's Germany in France, Spain and Russia before returning to post-war Germany to help in the founding of the GDR.

The Deputy also known in English as *The Representative*, this controversial 1963 play by German playwright Rolf Hochhuth portrays Pope Pius XII as having failed to speak out against the Holocaust. The play was first performed in West Berlin in 1963 then widely translated and performed throughout Europe. It was first performed in the GDR in 1966.

Then mine eyes fill with tears / my heart with sweet sorrow / farewell... farewell... farewell... later lines from the 1855 folk song by Adalbert Keller, as remembered by Lene.

There are no supreme saviours these lines are from 'The Internationale', by Eugène Pottier, a French revolutionary hymn adopted internationally as the marching song of the revolutionary proletariat, emphasising atheism and self-salvation for the working classes and the oppressed. In the GDR it ranked alongside the National Anthem.

Two Rowing a Boat a poem by Reiner Kunze (b. 1933). This East German dissident poet left the SED following the Prague Spring of 1968, was expelled from the GDR Writers' Union in 1974 and defected to West Germany in 1977.

What may stifle us... a 1985 quote from GDR author Volker Braun.

When everything comes to life again... a German folk song dating from 1855, written by Adalbert Keller.